About the Author

Malcolm Blair-Robinson was born in Sussex shortly before the outbreak of World War 2. His Grandfather was an East Prussian whose family had lived for centuries on an estate on the Baltic Coast. His unusual family history has provided inspiration for his writing.

He spent much of his working life in the insurance industry before fulfilling his ambition to write. Following the publication of his first two novels there was a gap of twelve years while he devoted his life to the care of his youngest daughter, who suffered lifelong illness. After her sad death he has returned to writing. He has five surviving children, four adult and one teenager. He has one grandchild.

I0677632

Stanislaw's Crossing

A St John Whilloe Mystery

Malcolm Blair-Robinson

Other titles by this author:
Downfall
The Judas Cross
A Gift of Treason

Published 2008 by arima publishing

www.arimapublishing.com

ISBN 978 1 84549 324 0

© Malcolm Blair-Robinson 2008

All rights reserved

This book is copyright. Subject to statutory exception and to provisions
of relevant collective licensing agreements, no part of this publication
may be reproduced, stored in a retrieval system, or transmitted in any
form or by any means, without the prior written permission of the
author.

Printed and bound in the United Kingdom

Typeset in Garamond 11/14

This book is sold subject to the conditions that it shall not, by way of
trade or otherwise, be lent, re-sold, hired out, or otherwise circulated
without the publisher's prior consent in any form of binding or cover
other than that which it is published and without a similar condition
including this condition being imposed on the subsequent purchaser.

In this work of fiction, the characters, places and events are either the
product of the author's imagination or they are used entirely fictitiously.
Any resemblance to actual persons, living or dead, is purely
coincidental.

Swirl is an imprint of arima publishing.

arima publishing
ASK House, Northgate Avenue
Bury St Edmunds, Suffolk IP32 6BB
t: (+44) 01284 700321

www.arimapublishing.com

CHAPTER ONE

I let the phone ring four times before I picked it up. It was best to appear busy.

"Mrs Michener is here to see you."

"Thank you, Janice, I will be along shortly."

I dropped the phone back on its rest. I looked at my diary, smart black leather with Whilloes 1986 in gold on the front. The day was blank save for an entry in Janice's hand at twelve noon: Mrs Michener.

The ringing of the telephone had broken the silence. For central London, my office is certainly silent. All I can hear is the gentle hissing of the water pumping through the central heating system. The block is seven floors high. I am on the seventh, at the back. I overlook the green of Lincoln's Inn, a legal campus embodying in its mellowed aspect all that is finest in the British tradition of justice, fair play and laws for the protection of the common man. Balance, enlightenment, truth. Yet I, who know the inner workings of the law, see humbug, bigotry, avarice.

I am not a lawyer, my brothers are. Gerard is now senior partner of the family firm, *Whilloes*, in whose palatial offices this family connection allows me to occupy, rent free, a modest room in the attic regions, way above the plush and leather of the partners' floor. Up here I am surrounded by crowded little cells occupied by harassed and overworked assistant solicitors who do the actual work commanding the extortionate fees demanded for a consultation in the measured opulence below.

My second brother, Carstairs Whilloe QC, is now quite senior in Chambers in the Temple. I say my brothers, but they aren't really, since they are of the Whilloe blood. I was adopted. Evidently, after the birth of Carstairs, my mother suffered an infection - well, I know she wasn't my mother, but I am going to call her such, otherwise it will be tedious - my mother suffered an infection, there was an operation so that there could be no more children. She insisted on a third, I have no idea why, so I was adopted when I was a few weeks old. I do not know who my parents are, and have never been interested to find out. If they didn't want me, there is not much point in knowing.

On my office door there is a small hand painted sign which says *St John Whilloe, Consultant.* My parents gave all their sons silly names. Nobody knows how to say mine anyway. It rhymes with Injun. I am not sure what *Consultant* means, but I like to think I am a crusader for just causes and a debunker of hypocrisy. In practise, I am a part time investigative journalist, free-lance, which is why I am part time, because I can never find enough debunking to keep me busy full time.

I became quite well-known about five years ago when I wrote a book exposing the doubtful methods of a City financier, which was serialised in one of the quality Sundays and helped to bring him down. But memories fade, and all but the City's inner circle have now forgotten the financier, let alone his nemesis. There have been other bits and pieces which have kept me going. There was something about pyramid selling which was used by World in Action, and I started a project investigating the process of laundering drugs money, but it became a bit scary so I dropped it.

The family do not approve of me, but to keep me out of undue mischief they provide this office, pay me a retainer and use me when they need information or research which is too dirty for smart lawyers to get mixed up in. I refuse to hang about in the shadows watching adulterers. I told Gerard I hadn't got a dirty enough mac. He didn't like that. I have tried writing a novel, but when I sent the first draft around to a few publishers, they all said it was crap, so I gave up. I am single, though a live-in deal, which lasted five years, ended a while ago.

To meet my visitor, I walked down the passage to a little office which Janice shares with too many filing cabinets and a sagging chesterfield with twanging springs that pinch your bum if you are careless about sitting yourself on it. Janice is included in the facility, though since I do not keep her busy, she does copy typing for the young sweatshop lawyers. I had no idea who Mrs Michener was or why Gerard had sent her to see me. This was quite usual. In spite of the fees he charged, he made his clients explain their problems to me. Sending a memo would have cost money.

I opened Janice's door with a flourish. Mrs Michener stood by the window. She had wisely avoided the chesterfield. She was under thirty, quite tall and very pretty. Her face was long, her nose straight, nearly too big but not quite. Loose auburn hair just touched her shoulders. She was wearing a short tweed coat over a wool dress. Everything was well cut. I could tell she had class.

She looked at me in surprise. I suppose a corduroy jacket and shaggy beard is not what she expected, even in the attics of *Whilloes*, especially not at their fees. Nevertheless she smiled and held out her hand. I gripped it gently and touched expensive rings. I led her to my office and settled her in the visitor's chair, leather, of the same vintage as the chesterfield, but less worn.

She sat, nervously, knees tight together, hands in lap clutching her bag. I sat behind the desk, pencil in hand ready to make notes. To try and ease her obvious tension I asked for her address and telephone number. She lived in a village in West Sussex in a substantial property not far from the church. I looked at her eyes. They were pale green, nearly grey, and sharp with fear.

"Tell me, Mrs Michener, how do you feel I can help you?"

The agitated hands turned the handbag over in her lap.

"I am not sure you can."

"Well, at least give me an opportunity to try."

She took a deep breath. "It's my husband..."

Oh God, I thought, a dirty mac project. I'll kill Gerard. He knows I won't do this.

"Your husband, Mrs Michener?"

"Yes, something strange is happening."

"Strange? In what way strange?"

"Well, it is rather difficult to explain. When I try to explain it, it sounds so silly."

I looked at the clock on the wall, an Edwardian Dent. It was twelve fifteen. This girl needed a drink.

"Mrs Michener, we are in no hurry. May I suggest we cross over the road and have a light lunch so that you can tell me your story in more relaxed surroundings? I can return to the office and make notes afterwards."

Her face lightened, and then once more became anxious.

"That's most awfully kind, but I really don't think I can put you to all this trouble."

"Think nothing of it, I have nobody else to see today anyway."

We took the lift to the ground floor, stopping in the plush sector to pick up an overfed partner. He beamed an oily smile at Mrs Michener and looked disapprovingly at me.

We left the building by the main entrance which opened onto High Holborn. Opposite was an establishment called the Wine Cellars, which contained an underground grill room, usually overcrowded, always hot, where the service was mostly slow and confused. There was, however, an upstairs restaurant on the first floor, where the ambience was altogether different. Bright and open with marble-topped tables on wrought iron legs, it specialised in fish and salads. The tables were well spaced and the waitresses cheerful.

We were early, there was plenty of choice, so we sat by the window. I ordered a bottle of Chablis. Mrs Michener was not concentrating, so I ordered for both of us. Potted shrimps and poached Scottish salmon. I was on expenses - *Whilloes* would pick up the tab. I kept the conversation to small talk until we were on our second glass of wine, when colour had appeared in her cheeks and she seemed calmer. I decided to dispense with formality.

"Before you begin, forget the Mr Whilloe stuff. Call me Jack."

She looked at me uncertainly. I detected a faint blush. She was not used to familiarity with strangers.

"I thought it said St John on your door?"

"It does, but it is silly. I prefer Jack." Actually, only two others called me Jack. One was Melissa.

She laughed. I felt we were getting somewhere.

"Very well, Jack!" A pause. Another little blush. "My name is Davina."

Christ! I might have guessed!

She tossed her head and her smile took on new warmth. Was she starting to flirt?

"You're very considerate. I know you are trying to make it easier for me. Let me try and tell you my story."

As Davina had said, her story was strange, yet I think not strange in the way she meant. The odd thing about it was there wasn't really any story at all. She explained that her husband, Martin, had decided to move into a rambling Victorian property which had once belonged to his grandfather, and which he had inherited from his father. The old man had died when he was a baby, but Martin had spent his childhood there. Davina thought it was too large, but nevertheless went along with him as the village was attractive and she herself had been brought up in the country.

The problem appeared to be that her husband's personality had changed almost immediately they had moved in. Instead of the congenial, life and soul of the party type she had married three years earlier, Martin had turned into a scheming and irritable pedant with whom she was finding it increasingly difficult to live. Whilst I had every sympathy for her, I could not see that this was a reason for consulting lawyers and hiring investigators unless divorce was the objective, which she made clear it was not.

"Where does your money come from?" I asked her. There was no point in beating around the bush.

She looked surprised. Clearly this was not a subject which often crossed her mind.

"Money? Oh! Yes. Money. Well, my family are quite comfortable and Martin has his business."

"Did he start it?"

"No, he inherited it from his father, but it was founded by his grandfather."

"The one who lived in the house originally?"

"Yes."

I wasn't sure I was getting anywhere. "What does the business do?"

"I don't really know. I sort of do. They make things."

Martin Michener's business colleagues clearly had no cause to be alarmed at the potential influence of his wife.

"Do you know what sort of things they make?"

"I think it is surgical instruments mostly, but I believe it includes knives, scissors and so on."

We had reached coffee. I had enjoyed the lunch, and Davina Michener was pleasant company. However, this was not an assignment but a false alarm. I thought I had better let her down gently.

"Davina, what you have told me is very interesting, and I am sure your husband's change of personality is very annoying, disturbing even, but I do not see that I am qualified to help you."

The girl looked at me anxiously. "Mr Whilloe, I mean Mr Gerard Whilloe, said you were good at research."

"Research? What kind of research do you mean?"

It was then we started to get to the meat of the story. It seemed that the Micheners had a funny past, and there was some connection with another family in the village named Mynot. Evidently, the Mynots owned thousands of acres of farmland and woods. There had been a quarrel, even a feud. Davina sensed hostility and disapproval from local people.

"What I would like you to do, Jack, is find out what all this is about. If we understand the past, we might be able to understand the change which seems to have taken over Martin and do something about it."

We talked further. Davina suggested I visit and stay at the house, but I felt this would arouse the ire of an already difficult Martin, so I said I would prefer to live out. Apparently, there was a woman in the village who let out a room on a paying guest basis from time to time. That sounded ideal. Surprisingly, Davina had the name and telephone number. Maybe she was more calculating than I thought.

We had now finished our third cup of coffee, and I had paid the bill. There was no point in returning to the office together, and I agreed to appear at Beechurst for dinner on the following Saturday. My cover was to be that of an author writing a novel and seeking seclusion. We did not discuss how I was supposed to have met Davina, but I assumed she would think of something.

We shook hands on the pavement in High Holborn before my new client climbed into a taxi and set off for Victoria. I suppressed an urge to kiss her on the cheek. It was the wine, but I had a feeling she would not have objected.

Wandering back to the office I thought of Melissa. We met at a reception, I can't remember for what or for whom, run by a trendy public relations firm. I was on a high at that point having just published my exposé of the suspect financier. Melissa was hardly known. She had started reading the news, but only local bulletins for some sub-section of one of the smaller companies up towards the Scottish border. She was bright-eyed and unused to London. She saw me as a door opener and was deft with the key. We slept together for the first time that night after a late dinner at a Chinese restaurant in Soho. She was fantastic in bed, but I wasn't much good because I was pissed. She moved in with me a few days later. It occurred to me afterwards she probably had nowhere else to go. She managed to get a job at the BBC, and, well, after that, there was no stopping her.

Back at the office, Janice detected the wine. She busied herself quickly to make a pot of tea. I had two days to prepare and sat at my desk to make a list. Clothes were not a problem. The whole lot would fit into a modest suitcase. Gerard was very disapproving of my wardrobe or lack of it, and once sent me to his tailor, a very exclusive little firm in Saville Row, even used by Royalty apparently. Gerard is a frightful creep. They made me three suits, a pinstripe, a grey and a tweed. The whole thing must have cost a couple of grand.

Anyway, when I looked at myself in them, they turned me into just the sort of person I did not want to be, so I took them down to the Oxfam shop and changed them for some worn stuff that I preferred. The woman running the place that day was astonished. She murmured that I appeared to be the same size as her husband. I told her to sell the suits to him for a tenner. It would do a bit of good all round, help the charity and promote hubby's career. He was an accountant apparently, so they were ideal.

That is how I got my corduroy jacket. Marvellous. I have worn it every day since. Now I looked down at it. Perhaps I should drop it in to the four-hour cleaners in the morning. There were rather a lot of food stains. When Gerard discovered what had happened to his suits he flew into a frightful rage and threatened to stop my retainer. I countered by saying that I would have to make up for the loss of income by writing an exposé of the legal profession, so he relented. You could tell we were not really brothers because we hated each other.

The tea arrived. I waited until it was half cold and drank it in one gulp. That's how I like it best. It was time to return to my flat in Bayswater, so I blew Janice a kiss and set off to catch the tube.

By the time I climbed the three flights to the flat, showered and started a beer, the social bonhomie brought on by the lunch had worn off. I began to think seriously about my new assignment. Instinctively I could tell that I had been dealt a much nastier hand than the facts so far revealed. Davina was the type who would have been brought up to understate rather than exaggerate, to be sensible and rational and show a stiff upper lip. If she had now been pushed to wasting a great deal of money with *Whilloes*, her fear must run much deeper than she had revealed to me. This husband of hers had something going on in the background, connected with the past. Whatever it was, it clearly was not good news.

CHAPTER TWO

On the Saturday morning I rose with enthusiasm and quite early. I was not due in Beechurst until late afternoon, which would give me time to check into my lodgings before going to the Micheners for dinner. I had that sense of adventure which always comes at the start of a new assignment, which is why I prefer my unpredictable lifestyle to the stuffy repetition most other people call security.

I busied myself with domestic obligations, tidying the flat and so on. I hate domestic muddle. I could not tell how long it would be before I returned, but I hate returning to confusion. I do not have milk or papers delivered, so there was nothing to cancel, and the day before I had arranged for the redirection of my mail to Beechurst. In the past, I had had the redirection to *Whilloes*, but that bastard Gerard read my letters, using the excuse that something might need attention. Now, I always have my post follow me to wherever I am going.

By eleven thirty I had shoved my suitcase, leather and old, a bargain picked up at a boot sale, into the back of the Morgan, put on my Australian stockman's coat festooned with capes, straps and fastenings, climbed into the cockpit of motoring nostalgia and roared off through South London in the direction of Sussex.

I say roared, but I exaggerate. I crawled along most of the time at less than walking pace, reflecting that when the original Morgans were made, long before the war, the journey I was making would have been much less hassle and a lot quicker. I used to have a Dyane, largely because if all you could do nowadays was to crawl about, there was really no point in having a powerful car. The trouble was that when one eventually made it to a motorway and got going, it took a long time to travel the bigger distances. So after I was in funds following the book, I invested in the Morgan. Second-hand, at low mileage, it was ideal. I loved it. Never put up the hood. Even in the wet. The stockman's coat kept me dry.

Finally I reached the M23, but when that fizzled out and became the A23 I turned off and decided to meander the rest of the journey through the byways. Beechurst is southeast of Midhurst, where Sussex is at its best, preserved by landed wealth.

I came upon a cosy pub and decided to stop for a beer and a ploughman's. This pub had not been modernised and still had the old public bar and saloon. I chose the former. I nodded at the locals who looked at me suspiciously, then sat in a corner quaffing real ale and munching cheese. The room was quite large. There was a pool table, nobody was playing, and a television set high above the bar, I imagine so that the regulars could watch the Saturday afternoon sport. It was news time. Melissa was reading it. The locals, only three of them, gnarled and ancient, stared upwards. I reckoned their attention was caught more by Melissa than what she was telling us about world affairs. I wondered if their imaginations, foggy with beery fumes, were undressing her. It would have surprised them to know that the stranger in the corner had seen her undress almost daily for five years. They should have been envious. It was always worth watching.

Melissa did not have class, but she had acquired style. She came from up north. Her father did something quite ordinary, I forget what. She had taken lessons in how to speak, and now had the neutral accent typical of newscasters. She spent a good bit of her considerable salary on expensive underclothes from Bond Street. The result was sensual and erotic rather than sexy and cheap. One old rustic muttered something into his beer which made the other two laugh. I could not hear what it was he said, but I guessed. It was time to return to the Morgan.

I still had plenty of time, so I decided to make a detour. Soon I was in perfect West Sussex countryside, the nostalgic images of which had appeared on countless calendars typifying England at its tranquil best. This was a countryside of money, mostly unspoiled by the windswept wastes of intensive farming methods. Here were fields and meadows of manageable size, hedges and woodlands, ancient, deciduous and virgin. Oak, beech and chestnut shimmering now in the afternoon sun. Their cloak of soft autumn gold worn with pride, as a reward for the fulfilment of another season, the completion of another cycle, and the foundation of a new renewal. The chill of the air told that the hovering gloom of winter would not be long deferred, yet now all was perfection. A sign pointed towards the Downland, marked *Public Footpath*. I left the Morgan in a gateway to a field and began to walk.

I wore stout shoes. I never economise with the feet. A great uncle, old Hubert Whilloe, had presented me with a pair of lasts at Lobbs for my twenty-first. Handmade, of perfect fit and quality, my shoes lasted forever and were still good when old, thus blending with my Oxfam wardrobe. I reached the brow, puffing. I was atop the downs with breathtaking views in almost all directions. There was no wind and few sounds, not even the hum of distant traffic as I was sufficiently off the beaten track. From somewhere in the fields below rose the throaty song of a labouring tractor. The barking of a dog, aimless but happy, echoed from beneath the dipping sun. I caught the strange and slightly sinister call of rooks circling above the tower of a village church, firm in its medieval simplicity, surrounded by its little clutch of houses, like a mother hen with chicks. Timeless, tranquil and certain.

Back in the car I felt refreshed and light-hearted. I tuned the radio to music and found a news bulletin by mistake. I listened to the usual stuff about Europe, the economy and starvation somewhere in Africa. Then suddenly, an extra item. There had been a murder. A young woman found dead in her home. Her name withheld until next of kin, etc., but the village was named. It was Beechurst. A chill ran up my spine. The lightness of spirit brought on by the Downland walk evaporated instantly. I gunned the Morgan and headed towards my destination with an increasing sense of foreboding.

A little over half an hour later I reached the village. Largely unspoiled, its properties huddled together along a narrow street within boundaries which had remained unchanged from medieval times. There had been no modern development, just a little in-filling of the odd plot here and there, some by the Victorians who had used the larger plots, and some post war.

I was looking for The Grange. That certainly sounded Victorian. I found it standing on its own at the end of the village, almost entirely concealed behind yew trees and laurel bushes. The shadow of its huge bulk was visible. It seemed to be of the worst sort of Victorian Gothic, probably a well-to-do merchant retiring to the country at the turn of the century, inspired by his admiration of St Pancras Station.

It was not the house itself that first caught my eye, but the collection of police vehicles, including one of those special caravans which they use as an incident room. This confirmed my worst fears. I stopped the Morgan at a distance and walked to the gate. This whole assignment had taken on a nasty aspect. I had not had much dealing with crime, and certainly did not expect clients to be murdered, especially not an attractive young girl in her own house before we had had an opportunity for a second meeting. A constable stood at the gate.

"Can I help you, Sir?"

"I am from the deceased's solicitors."

I waved a *Whilloes* visiting card at him. He gave me instructions to speak to the inspector inside the house. I rang the bell. A plain clothes officer opened the door. There were policemen everywhere. After I had explained, he went to fetch the inspector, who looked at me suspiciously. The shaggy beard and stockman's coat did not fit his image of a solicitor.

I explained again, this time using the cover that I had agreed with Davina. My family connection with her solicitors, *Whilloes*, had brought us into contact socially, and I had casually mentioned that I had wanted to hide in order to complete my novel. She had suggested Beechurst and found suitable lodgings. I had heard of the tragedy on the car radio and realised the worst when I had seen the police cars.

Chief Inspector Bridgenorth, I learned his name later, listened attentively. I hoped he would not detect that much of what I had said was lies. He told me there was nothing to be done for the moment. I asked how Mr Michener had taken the news. He looked at me but did not reply. Did the Inspector yet know how Davina had died and was there a motive? Bridgenorth's brown eyes were steady. His dark hair was cut quite short. His florid features had a hint of youthful good looks. He wore a mac which was surprising. I had thought detectives in macs went out with the B-movies. Was he willing to part with information, however general, or would he tell me to piss off?

"Battered to death with a poker. Robbery appears the motive. There is evidence of valuables missing. It very much looks as if she disturbed an intruder. That's all we know for the moment."

I thanked him and made my way back to the Morgan, reflecting on the coincidence that my frightened client had been battered to death by a passing burglar. Whatever that girl had been frightened of when she sought my help, it was not passing burglars. Davina dead! This was shocking. I felt dismayed and almost headed back to London, but I owed it to her at least to hang around for a day or two and watch developments.

I found Briar Cottage near the centre of the village. It was a double fronted Victorian in-fill, but cosy and welcoming. Mrs Richardson, my landlady, was just as I expected. About thirty- five, two or three inches over five foot, with a comfortable figure neatly encased in twin set and tweed skirt. The neat hair was dark, and I had the impression her eyes were brown. There was a daughter, Jennifer, about twelve, who was a younger replica of her mother. My room overlooked the garden. It was not huge but big enough, with a table by the window which Susan, she asked that I use her first name, had moved into the room especially for my writing. I thanked her and returned the compliment of the name, but she seemed to find St John rather intimidating, and for the time being, at least, stuck to Mr Whilloe. I did not offer Jack. That was kept for my intimates. Strange how I had accepted Davina as one of them.

The bathroom was right next door to my bedroom. It incorporated the lavatory, so I would have to remember not to fall asleep in the bath. Susan explained that in the event of crisis, there was an outside WC, but this establishment was evidently rather draughty in the winter months. After I had been shown all these domestic arrangements, my new landlady took me into the kitchen for a cup of tea. We spoke in hushed tones of the horrific event at The Grange. Susan appeared quite moved.

"She was such a nice girl. I knew her quite well. We always talked when we met in the village, and we were both on the committee that organised the fete and things like that. Just goes to show," she went on, "you're not safe anywhere now, not even in a little village like this. Especially not in these big houses full of valuables, tucked away out of sight. It's just those sort of places the modern criminals make for!"

Susan shot me a glance as she sipped her tea. There was an openness about her face which appealed to me. She went on earnestly.

"To tell you the truth, with a murder so close to home, I am thankful that Jenny and me will not be on our own for the time being, now that you're staying with us." I laughed the sort of nervous laugh that has nothing to do with humour.

Later, when I was unpacking my suitcase, there was a tap at the door. I turned. Susan was in the doorway holding a note.

"I did not mention it earlier, but this came for you this morning, shortly after breakfast."

I took the envelope. I slit it open untidily with my thumb. Inside, on heavy blue paper, was a note. It said,

Mr Whilloe
I have discovered something amazing which you need to know before you come to dinner tonight. Please meet me outside the west door of the church at five tonight.
Regards
Davina Michener

Susan was still standing in the doorway. I folded the note.

"I was supposed to be going there to dinner tonight. It was just confirming the arrangements."

"Oh," she said. She turned and went downstairs.

The note was odd. *Mr Whilloe?* I thought we were on Jack terms.

I looked out of the window. It was now dark. I saw myself reflected, a touch wide-eyed, I thought, from the shock. So Davina had found out something, something she had to tell me about, and before she could do this, perhaps when she returned from delivering the note to this house, she had disturbed a burglar and been battered to death. Each of those facts seemed plausible on its own, but they did not join together properly. It would be interesting to see whether the police could find any trace of the burglar, but behind the brutal killing of this unfortunate girl loomed the shadow of the husband of whom she was terrified.

I looked at my watch. It was ten to five. On impulse I decided I would keep the appointment by the west door of the church. It was a strange place to meet. There may have been some significance in its choice. Churchyards hide a lot of history. Maybe Davina wanted to show me something there. I took a flashlight from the bottom of my case, a powerful instrument made of cast aluminium with a long handle containing four batteries. In an emergency it would make an effective cosh, better than a poker even. I shuddered and slid it into an inside pocket of my coat. In the hall I called to Susan.

"Just going out for some air."

She hurried from the kitchen.

"You'll need this." I was handed a newly cut key. "You will want to be able to come and go as you please." Susan smiled. What is she expecting me to get up to, I wondered?

Outside the temperature had dropped but the sky was clear. The church was not far. Parts of it, including the tower, were very old. Probably Norman. There were some later additions. As I walked up the path, the doorway ahead me, clearly the one most frequently used, faced south. The west door must be to the left. I found it set into a deep porch, across which was an iron grill locked with a rusty padlock. This entrance was barely ever used. So why should we meet here? Nearby the gnarled trunk of a yew, hundreds of years old, reached with twisted branches for the sky.

I switched on the flashlight. There was nothing behind the iron grill in the porch except leaves and cobwebs. On either side alcove seats looked rotten and unsafe. I could imagine a heavy curtain behind the door to keep draughts from chilling the ankles of the worshippers beyond. There was a half moon, and I could make out the leaning shadows of the headstones, a mute but eloquent testament to the generations of Beechurst folk, whose brief passage of life had now given way to the superior forces of eternity.

Then I saw them. Lined up abreast as if to greet me, or perhaps to mock. Stanley Michener 1880-1956, Eva Michener 1891-1953, Arnold Michener 1911-1988, and finally, Katherine Michener 1919-1984. The stones of heavy granite stood true at the head of each grave, which was kept neat and trim. The aspect was more Highgate than a country churchyard. There was an ostentation and assertiveness that seemed out of keeping with the gentle flow of life in a Sussex village.

Further into the churchyard and somewhat to the right, another clutch of stones, more modest, softened by mosses and lichen, marked the resting places of the Mynots. The inscriptions were faint and hard to read. Unlike the military precision of the row of Micheners, the Mynot's burial area was less well organised. The memorials leaned towards each other in a friendly, intimate sort of way, which suggested a family warmth at peace with itself.

I stood and wondered what Davina wished to show me here. It could be no coincidence that these graves were a meeting place. She had discovered something about these families. I shivered. Soon she, too, perhaps, would lie here, although nowadays cremations were more in vogue. I thought of Davina, young and frightened in my office. I thought of her again, at lunch, becoming more animated with wine. I thought of her getting into the taxi, and how I had resisted an urge to kiss her. Now I wish I had. Perhaps we would have met again. Perhaps I could have prevented her murder. One thing was for sure. My assignment was over. Dead people cannot pay. This was a police job.

When I let myself into Briar Cottage, Susan was waiting for me in the hall.

"Mr Michener telephoned."

"For me?"

"Just a few minutes ago. He asked that you call back."

She gave me the number. The phone, a peculiar and rather vulgar reproduction of an Edwardian model, stood on a small table in the hall.

A quavering voice which must have come from some elderly manservant, answered, "Michener House, who is it?"

I was taken aback by this strange greeting. I responded in kind.

"Whilloe."

"Wait a moment." There was a clatter as the phone was put down, and another a few moments later as it was picked up.

"Good evening, Mr Whilloe. It's kind of you to return my call. This is Martin Michener. I believe we are expecting you for dinner this evening?"

I fought to gather my scattering wits.

"For dinner? But naturally I had imagined, in view of what has happened... I mean, I am most awfully sorry..."

"Shall we say seven thirty? We dine at eight. That will leave us time for champagne first. The best drink for death!"

The line went dead. It was just as well. I was speechless. Susan was still hovering in the kitchen doorway. I had not really discussed meals. I was not sure what the arrangements were.

"Apparently I am expected there to dinner. It seems rather unusual. I won't be late," I added as I turned my back. I sensed disappointment. Susan clearly met too few men.

Upstairs I considered changing into a blazer and flannels, the only other clothes I had brought, but I decided the corduroy jacket would do. It was not very funereal, but if the evening were to be spent quaffing champagne, it did not seem to matter. If Martin Michener had murdered his wife, he was keeping a very cool head.

Later, as I approached The Grange on foot, I noticed a small police car parked on the verge close to the front gate. The caravan was in darkness, but in the car the interior light revealed a constable seated inside. He appeared to be writing something in his notebook. I supposed all comings and goings were to be recorded. I had better be careful with the champagne. It would not do to leave with an unsteady gait.

The bell was the type you pull rather than push. Somewhere deep inside the house there was an eerie jangling. There was no light in the porch, but some reflection of the hall light came through the coloured glass panel set in the door. A shadow loomed slowly forward. I heard the sound of bolts being drawn back. The door opened to reveal a stooped figure, presumably the manservant to whom I had spoken on the phone. He was formally dressed in a dinner jacket. He looked disdainfully at the stockman. I took it off while he closed the door and shot the bolts.

The hall was hideous. Heavy oak panelling with ornamental carving and fretwork covered the walls. The dim lighting came from swan neck wall lights with glass globes of a style normally reserved for public houses near railway stations. Alarming hunting trophies glared at me malevolently with their glass eyes. Wild boar and a huge elk, as well as deer and foxes. The wheezing retainer took my coat.

"This way, Mr Whilloe."

As we approached a door, it opened. Martin Michener extended his hand in welcome.

"Mr Whilloe, how very good of you to come."

He was about my height with short dark hair, a prominent nose and a small, though not receding, chin. His face was slightly out of balance because the top half was larger than the lower part. His eyes were dark and rather strange, but quite why I could not then tell. He was dressed in a well cut tweed jacket of a very loud check, together with cavalry twill trousers and suede shoes. I felt comfortable in corduroy, in spite of the disdain of the relic, who now hovered in the hall with my coat on his arm. My host turned to him.

"Thank you, Elderflower, I can manage now."

This was scarcely believable. Elderflower? What sort of a name was that? My host took my arm and led me towards the roaring fire.

"I am afraid we cannot use the drawing room as the police sealed it, together with the main bedroom upstairs. Fortunately there are plenty of other rooms in this house, so it does not put us to much inconvenience."

Inconvenience? Surely if one's wife has been murdered that very day, domestic convenience would be the last thing on one's mind, even if one had done the deed oneself? Martin poured champagne into exquisite flutes, one of which he handed to me. His hands were broad with short fingers but, I suspected, very strong.

"Let us drink a toast to life."

This was weird. I raised my glass and sipped. It was time to say something.

"You are coping remarkably well with your tragedy?"

"There is nothing to cope with. Davina is dead. One has to cope with people when they are alive, but when they are dead, it is over." Martin waved me to an enormous armchair. "Make yourself comfortable."

I gulped champagne. No wonder Davina had turned in desperation to *Whilloes*. I could scarcely imagine how this gentle young girl had managed to live at all with this creepy man in a mausoleum of a house with the ghostly Elderflower shuffling about in the background.

I looked about me. The room was high and gloomily lit. The walls were lined with books from floor to ceiling, many leather bound, all old. Few, I imagined, which would provide light reading or entertainment. Those close to me appeared to have titles which indicated that they were either in German or Polish. The bay window housed a monstrous desk of over-carved oak with legs fashioned into massive clawed feet, which, if given life, looked as if they would have the power to sunder the hide of an elephant.

As I sat in the great chair I had the illusion I was growing smaller, whilst the book-lined walls leaned inwards to grip me in a cloying, menacing embrace. Martin was talking in strange disconnected tones, distant and echoing and hard to fathom. I wondered if the champagne were drugged. More, I felt that my reason, overwhelmed by the evil atmosphere, was in flight from my mind. I tried to claw it back, and in so doing had the sensation of being dragged by the string of a gigantic kite towards the edge of a windy cliff.

The strain was broken by Elderflower announcing in the doorway that dinner was served. We crossed the hall to the dining room. Here again, the gloomy, oppressive decor offered no relief from the strange unwelcoming atmosphere. I struggled to get a grip of myself. I was not at all prepared for this experience. Had Davina been alive, would things have felt different, I wondered? Was it the house, or was it Martin who was the source of this foreboding? Unexpectedly, the food was delicate, beautifully prepared and well presented. We began with mushrooms in wild garlic, the latter welcome protection against the lurking vampires of my fevered imaginings. Someone knew how to cook and I fancied it was not Elderflower. Wines were of the finest, but I drank sparingly.

Gradually, a sense of well-being returned and conversation between us flowed more easily. The family business had been established before the Hitler War, Martin told me. His grandfather had been in the knives and surgical instruments business in Poland, and though not Jewish himself, had married a Jewish girl. When the Nazis took power in Germany, he brought his wife and son over to England, established his business, and eventually became a British citizen. The breakthrough came when he developed a range of instruments for field hospitals and surgery at the scene of battle. These were purchased in vast quantities to equip the forces, and his fortune was made.

When Martin's father took over, the business had been diversified into locks, security and anti-theft devices. Michener Security, through its trade name MicSec, was amongst the household names in this field, but I had not previously connected it. According to Martin, this was now the major arm of business.

I asked about the house. Evidently the grandfather, Stanley Michener, who had changed his name from Stanislaw and something Polish which I could not pronounce, much less spell, had bought the property quite cheaply at the end of the war and spent much time and energy renovating it. He restored it to its former glory, adding an undoubted East European flavour. I remembered how Davina had said that Martin's personality had changed when he moved into The Grange. I asked him when he had taken it over.

"My grandfather left it to my father, and he to me. My father modernised it but I have restored it to exactly the way it was in my grandfather's day."

I was surprised. Why should a young man, rich and successful, want to live in a sort of Siberian hunting lodge?

It was over coffee, served in the oppressive library, that Martin said something really strange. The tottering Elderflower had laid out the cups and saucers, and I had remarked on the excellence of the meal. Martin had explained that it was Elderflower's daughter who did the cooking. Apparently she was married and her husband looked after the garden. I asked Martin whether he had ever met his grandfather.

There came a rather cold reply. "Only as a baby. I have no recollection. He was nearly dead. The dead are the past. The living are the future."

It was just after this that I detected the creepy atmosphere returning, so I decided it was time to go. As I rose to offer thanks, my eye was caught by something on the desk which I had missed in my befuddled state before dinner. It was a copy of my book, *Financing Fraud.* Martin saw that I had seen it.

"I read it with interest." He looked straight at me. "From cover to cover." There was something threatening about his tone I did not like.

He walked across the room towards me, just as the leaning Elderflower appeared in the doorway with my coat.

"I shall look forward to reading your new book. I hope you will autograph me an early copy!"

Martin took my hand between both of his. His hands were dry but ice cold. I shivered and left. As the front door shut behind me and the sound of the bolts echoed in my ears, I made a decision. I was going to find out what had happened to Davina. If Martin had killed her I would see he paid the price with his freedom. A voice told me that this was the responsibility of the police, and that I was a fool to kid myself that I could do better, but adrenalin had flooded my stubborn brain and I was no longer willing to let go. As I stepped into the road I saw the constable jot a note into his book. I inclined my head in greeting and muttered beneath my breath, "At your service, St John Whilloe, Private Eye." When my back was turned I chuckled. This could, in its own macabre way, be rather fun.

CHAPTER THREE

Susan and Jennifer were probably asleep by the time I reached Briar Cottage that night. Anyway, the house was in darkness, save for an outside light to guide me up the path and another on the landing to light up the stairs. I restricted bathroom activities to cleaning my teeth and climbed into a bed which I found surprisingly comfortable.

For some time I lay awake, my mind awash with questions for which it had no answer. The clammy atmosphere of The Grange stayed with me as I shivered and drew my knees to my chest for warmth. Eventually I became drowsy and slipped into a sleep of confused and meaningless dreams.

I awoke to a sharp frost and a cup of early morning tea brought to my room by Jennifer.

"Mummy is doing a cooked breakfast. It will be ready in half an hour, and she says if you want a bath there is plenty of hot water."

I arrived punctually at the breakfast table sweet and clean, having shampooed not only my hair but my beard as well. In front of Jennifer, Susan and I kept the conversation away from murders as we all tucked into bacon and eggs.

Outside the bright sun melted the frost, but the forecast was for a cold day because of wind from the east. Nevertheless I decided to spend it out of doors to organise my confused thoughts. When she heard my plans, Susan offered to prepare a packed lunch. I said I would call in at a pub for a ploughman's, but she cautioned that it was Sunday. All the pubs would be full of unsuitables, though I fancied I was an unsuitable myself. I relented and was later handed a plastic box containing a picnic. There was also a flask of coffee. Susan was a very precise person. She rummaged in a cupboard under the stairs and produced a knapsack into which she stuffed the refreshments.

"Now they will be portable if you decide to walk."

I thanked her. It was good to be waited on like this.

The Morgan and I made for the Downs once again. I parked near a footpath and climbed to the top. The air was perfect and the view breathtaking. This seemed a far cry from the strange atmosphere of The Grange. I wondered if Davina was in heaven. If so, it could not be much of an improvement on this. The blue sky, the sharp crisp air and the soft autumn colouring uplifted my spirit, used as it was to city dwelling, and I arrived back at Briar Cottage in time for dinner with a clear mind and a good humour.

Susan had thoughtfully deferred the main meal until evening. We sat in the dining room using the best china and cutlery. The table was immaculate and I took care to avoid spills. Susan's cooking was safe rather than inspired, but there was a bottle of Beaujolais which helped lighten the atmosphere as we exchanged the news of the day.

I talked of the countryside and the colours, but Susan had altogether more useful information. The communications system of the village was now in full swing, disseminating every detail of the sad events at The Grange. Jennifer seemed to have even more news than her mother, so there was clearly no need to shield her from the worst.

Davina had been killed by a single blow to the back of the head from a heavy brass poker, part of the set beside the fireplace at The Grange.

"The murderer must have been very strong. The blow bashed Mrs Michener's head right in," volunteered Jennifer. Her mother winced.

Elderflower's daughter, Rosa, had gone to Chichester shopping, and her husband Joseph, a Hungarian who had fled the 1956 uprising, was way down at the bottom of the huge garden and saw and heard nothing. Old Elderflower was in the house, but he said he had fallen asleep in the rocking chair in his room, which was apparently on the lower ground floor facing from the back. His duties were limited to answering calls and waiting at table. Normally, when there was someone in the house, the doors were left unlocked, so it would have been very easy for the burglar to gain entry. Martin had been at the family's London flat overnight and was not expected until mid-afternoon. There was to be an inquest in Chichester on Tuesday. It was expected to be adjourned, but the funeral had been set for the following Friday.

When I reached my room later, feeling somewhat overfed, the apple crumble had been especially good, I thought through the next steps. Tomorrow morning I would revisit the churchyard and see in daylight if I could find any clues. After that, I would drive to London. I was beginning to sense that I would find some answers to the many unanswered questions there, and I had an idea where to look. I made a few pages of notes before turning out the light.

As I lay cocooned in the soft duvet, I thought of the neat and ordinary Susan and compared her with the glamorous Davina. They came from different worlds, yet shamefully I realised that my world was nearer Davina's. In Briar Cottage there was a cosy home. Although just the two of them, Susan and Jennifer were a family. They shared everything together. The Grange was just a house, a frightful one at that.

In some ways it was not that different to Messamer Hall, the headquarters of the Whilloe clan, where I had spent my early life, or rather part of it, because at the age of eight, like my stepbrothers, I was sent to a horrible boarding school in Hampshire. At thirteen I moved to something far worse, a public school famous throughout the world as representing the apex of one of the finest education systems available, but I never saw it that way. To me it was like being confined to a physical and mental prison. Physical, because one suffered absurd traditions, outmoded concepts and physical abuse. Mental, because I was forced to take part in a learning process designed to ensure that I would always conform to and preserve the perceived order of things, which a more enlightened regime should have educated me to challenge.

I went home in the holidays to the same rules and traditions. There was certainly care and affection, but not real love, because to show emotion would have been to undermine all that was strongest and finest. The family loved itself as a group, loved its house, loved its possessions, loved its history and loved its position in the community and in society. But its individual members were incapable of loving each other in the same way as Susan and her daughter. I had detected something of this from Melissa, who talked of her happy and carefree childhood often. There may have been shortages in her family and money had to be counted, but there was real warmth of a sort that I had not experienced. This was not because I was adopted. I was treated no differently to my brothers.

As I became drowsy my thoughts drifted to Melissa. I saw her standing there beside the bed, late from the studio, sensuous with expensive perfume and soft, secret silk, her kisses deep and tasting of wine, her touch light, but expert. Slowly I sank into sleep, but not without a tinge of regret for pleasures now past.

The following morning the routine at Briar Cottage was different. Jennifer had to set off early for school, although she dutifully brought me early morning tea first, but by the time I arrived downstairs, she had gone. I declined her mother's offer of a cooked breakfast. I could tell that Susan's concept of looking after a man was to fatten him, but I had trouble enough keeping fit as it was. I went to the churchyard and gazed at the line of reposing Micheners, searching for clues and thinking that in daylight their plot looked even more Highgate.

Suddenly a voice behind me said, "Apparently they can live for up to two thousand years."

I turned to face the vicar, identified by his dog collar and a somewhat donnish aspect. Very Oxford, I thought. Youthful middle age.

"Two thousand years!" I exclaimed. "Are they vampires?"

The vicar roared with laughter. "No, no! I mean the tree." I was standing under the yew.

He wore a tweed jacket over a home knitted pullover and flannels. His manner was engaging as he stretched out a hand.

"Neville Balcombe. I'm the vicar. I believe you are St John Whilloe, the author?"

We exchanged pleasantries. I was rather flattered by his description.

"Would you like to look around the church?"

It seemed good manners to accept the offer. Anyway, vicars know things about the village and he may have information. I listened to talk of chancel windows, carved screens and hammer beam roofs, nodding sagely as if I were taking it all in. Churches to me were cold draughty places with hard seats and acoustics which made it inadvisable to allow anything to happen which may make a noise. I discovered this whilst at prep school at the age of eleven, when I received four of the best in the Headmaster's study after morning service for being unable to control my bottom. The fact that most of the school were in uncontrollable giggles throughout the sermon undoubtedly influenced the severity of the punishment.

I detected that the tour of the church was a ploy by Balcombe to break the ice. Eventually he said, "Bad business at The Grange. Always sad when a parishioner dies. Much worse when it's a young girl, and almost unthinkable when it turns out to be murder."

I nodded. "It is through her kindness that I am here in Beechurst."

The vicar looked at me. "Really?"

I explained how I had met Davina socially in London and discussed the new book I was writing and how she had fixed up my digs at Susan's.

"How strange. She always said she would never go to London because she hated it so. She was a very country person, having been brought up here on the estate."

It was my turn to be puzzled. "Estate?"

"Well, perhaps that's a rather grand term, but it's such a huge farm."

"Farm? Which farm is that?"

"Haw Farm, the Mynot's place."

"The Mynots? Was Davina a Mynot?"

"Yes, of course. Didn't you know?"

I must have looked surprised. A convincing liar needs to do his research. Balcombe suggested a coffee at the vicarage. We could then have a chat, and anyway, his wife was keen on authors and would like to meet me.

I followed him through the churchyard in something of a daze. I distinctly remembered Davina talking of a feud between the Micheners and the Mynots. She gave the impression she had never lived in Beechurst before she and Martin moved into The Grange, yet it turned out she was a Mynot all along. Why would she conceal this from me?

The vicarage was a charming Queen Anne house, not too large, but confident with its bold, well-angled proportions. Mrs Balcombe was county. Her cashmere and pearls spoke for a deeper purse than the one provided by her husband's calling. I guessed she was not yet forty. She was clearly used to visitors popping in and out, and probably lived in a state of half-preparedness and continuous expectation. She bustled off to organise the coffee.

Contrary to the vicar's observation in the church, she seemed little interested in me.

Balcombe took me to his study. I was right about Oxford. He was a rowing blue and his oar hung from the wall. There were plenty of other mementos and photographs from school and student days, denoting progress and achievement. A crucifix, rather sensitively carved out of sycamore, was his only trophy for being a country vicar. He had been well selected for Beechurst. He fitted the tone of the village exactly, but I suspected he hoped for better things. I had little doubt that his wife did, and I was sure she put in a considerable effort behind the scenes to achieve the goal of occupying a bishop's palace somewhere one day.

We sat in homely chintz in front of an electric fire, which my host switched on as the room was rather chilly. I could see a night storage heater in the corner but no sign of pipes or radiators to denote central heating. That could be a considerable snag in a property of this sort in winter. I waited while Balcombe lit his pipe, as his wife brought in coffee on a tray. She did not stay. Evidently my visit was treated as business. Clearly the talk of her interest in authors was a ploy to lure me in, or else she thought I was so bad a writer as to not be worth the time of day. Anyway, it was becoming clear that Balcombe was dying to gossip.

"Such a tragedy to have this awful murder. We shall miss Davina. She was really the backbone of village life. As I think I mentioned earlier, she was very much into country things, horses and so on."

He offered me a biscuit which I declined with a shake of the head.

"Wasn't there a rift between the Mynots and the Micheners?" I ventured.

"Oh yes. Dreadful. It went on for years. The families were finally brought together when Martin and Davina married."

Balcolmbe wanted to talk. I decided to go for it. "What was the rift about?"

"Ah, my dear fellow, you don't know?"

"No, I wasn't close enough. Davina mentioned vaguely there had been a rift, but that was all."

Balcombe took several sips of coffee and some deep puffs at his pipe. He blew smoke from his mouth and nose, and at one point I thought from his ears, but this must have been an illusion. When he had stoked himself with sufficient caffeine and nicotine, he set forth on his narrative. It was quite a tale.

He confirmed that old Stanley Michener had bought The Grange for a song just before the end of the war. It had stood empty for some years before being occupied by troops and was in a poor state of repair. At that time nobody wanted big houses because of the cost of heating and the end of the era of servants. At first, the village treated him with great suspicion. He was not only a war profiteer, which was bad enough, but a foreigner as well which was shocking.

Stanley was shrewd, however, and anticipated his social difficulties. His wife Eva was charming, and their only son, Arnold, who was in his mid-thirties when the war ended, was something of a hero having fought both in the regular army and behind enemy lines. He was decorated several times, and when he left the forces, held the acting rank of Brigadier General. He was strikingly handsome in a dark, mid-European sort of way, an outstanding horseman and a crack shot. Women of all ages in the village and from all social backgrounds soon fell in love with him whether they were married or not, but whilst he flirted and dallied, his interests lay elsewhere.

Meanwhile, his father used his money discreetly for various improvement projects in the locality, particularly the church, to which he gave a substantial sum for a new roof and other works of restoration. Gradually the family was accepted into the old and close fabric of village life.

Eventually Arnold married, but his wife, Katherine, was not a local. It was generally thought that she did not really enjoy the country, and the newlyweds set up in London. They were married in 1949, when Katherine was only twenty and Arnold little short of forty, but surprisingly, years passed before there were any children. It was said there were one or two miscarriages and it was not until 1961 that Katherine gave birth to Martin.

Stanley's wife, Eva, died, and he scandalised everyone by marrying his secretary, Dorothy Skillette, a girl in her twenties when he was in his early seventies. It was at this point that the feud developed. The Mynots had owned the land around the village for generations and had become a large family with various branches and members. It seemed that one of them, a young man called Titus, made a beeline for Stanley's young bride. Stanley fell ill not long after the marriage with some form of cancer, and in his weakened state was not in a position to protect his marital interests.

Eventually the bride became pregnant, but the nature of Stanley's illness, let alone his age, precluded all possibility that he could be the father. A scandal erupted. Stanley summoned Titus and accused him of violating his wife, a charge which he hotly denied. Solicitors in the county were quite busy for a time, and damages were said to have been paid by the Micheners to the Mynots for alleged slanders. Though enfeebled physically, Stanley's rage knew no bounds. He banished his wife and started divorce proceedings, but died before his petition could be heard.

It was shortly before the time of the supposed affair that he persuaded Arnold and Katherine to give up their home in London and come and live with him at The Grange. The house was vast. There was no shortage of space, and he probably thought that Katherine would be company for his young wife. It was when living at The Grange that Katherine became pregnant, and had the circumstances been different, life for the two young wives, in the big house with their babies, could have been ideal.

Balcombe told his story well, with a lot of little anecdotes which I have not bothered to record. He took pleasure in telling the tale, though he was wise to caution me that most of his information was second hand, since the events had all taken place well before he became vicar of Beechurst.

"What happened to Titus?" I asked.

"Oh, he settled down and helps to run the family farms."

"What was Davina's relationship to him?"

"She was his niece."

This was a surprise.

"What happened to Stanley's young wife?"

"I'm afraid I'm not quite sure about that," replied Balcombe. "You see, she was not local, so the communications break down somewhat. She came from Lincolnshire. I think her family was quite well-to-do, but they rather cut her off when she married Stanley. When he threw her out, she had fallen between two stools, so to speak. Local legend has it that she lived in genteel, but rather modest circumstances outside Lincoln. I think she died a couple of years ago. A stroke or something."

"And the baby?"

"I imagine she must have brought it up, but Titus Mynot steadfastly refused to acknowledge that the child was his."

I looked at the clock on the chimney piece. It was nearly eleven thirty. Balcombe would go on gossiping all day. He had given me as much as I could take in, and I wanted to make my trip to London. I thanked him for his hospitality. It was fortunate that he so enjoyed talking of scandal that he never thought to ask why I was interested.

I took the Morgan to the M23 at speed, and then drove up to town as fast as I could. I was considerably perplexed. Instead of answering questions, my contacts were creating new ones. The impression Davina had created for me was quite different to the reality of her life described by Balcombe.

I parked in Lincoln's Inn Fields. There are always meters free, as the charges are so exorbitant. I no longer walked through the little park, which had become a cardboard city for the homeless. A disgraceful commentary on the values of modern society. I walked instead around three sides on the pavement. As I caught sight of those muffled and hopeless people I realised I hated politicians even more than lawyers.

I caught Gerard just before he went to lunch. As usual, his tone was disapproving.

"I gather from Janice you've debunked to Sussex. What are you up to?"

I ignored his question and asked one of my own. "Has Mrs Michener paid in advance for my services?"

"Who?"

"Davina Michener."

"I don't know what you are talking about."

Hastily I explained.

"Sorry St John, you've got your wires crossed. She never came to you through me. We don't even act for the Micheners." He looked at me with his heavy lidded eyes, narrowed and inquisitive. "Is she anything to do with the woman who was murdered the other day?"

I was already half way out of the door as I replied, "She *is* the woman, dammit."

The meter was good for two hours. I found a taxi and told the driver to take me to Blackfriars, to the headquarters of one of the popular Sunday newspapers. I was beginning to smell a rat, a very big rat indeed, and I needed information fast.

At the desk I asked for the previous day's edition. This was produced without difficulty. I skimmed the pages for details of the Beechurst murder, which had taken place on the day before publication. It was quite a big item on one of the inner pages, complete, as I suspected, with a photograph of the victim. A snapshot taken at a farm show or something, not very clear, but clear enough. I had never set eyes on this woman in my life.

CHAPTER FOUR

In a turmoil at this new twist in a gathering intrigue, I took the taxi to a little pub in an alley off Queen Victoria Street. It was now, more than ever, important to discover some proof for my theory that Martin Michener had murdered his wife, the real Davina. I might then discover the identity of the girl who came to see me in my office, and why she had persuaded me to set up temporary home in Beechurst on an errand of lies.

In my confusion I had an idea. If Martin had faked the burglary to cover his murder of the real Davina, he would need to follow it through properly. The jewellery and other items stolen must find their way into the system as if taken by professionals. The police would presumably be keeping a sharp lookout for them. There could not be many fences who would handle this sort of merchandise, and probably fewer still when there was a murder involved. I knew just the person to give me some names.

At the Iron Duke, Paddy Flynn was sitting in his usual seat in a tiny alcove to the left of the window. It was a fixed seat like a church pew, with a table, also fixed, in front of it. Two glasses stood before him. One was a pint jug nearly filled with Yorkshire bitter, the other was small and empty. It would have contained Jack Daniels. I once chided him for not drinking Guinness, but he said for an Irishman it was too obvious.

Paddy was a mixture of private detective and police informer who moved easily with key people of the underworld. Sometimes he informed on them, sometimes he passed disinformation to the police on their behalf to send the investigators down a false trail. I used him as my sub-contracting peeping Tom, for assignments which had a dirty mac aspect. He was also adept at finding things out, having investigative skills that should have put him in the higher ranks of police. But he was like me. He would not conform to convention or discipline. He had to be his own man. He ate little and drank a lot, yet I never saw him drunk. He was taller than me and slimmer, with brown hair growing thin. His watery eyes and florid complexion were evidence of the fondness for alcohol.

The Iron Duke was his office. He was in attendance in the alcove every day from eleven to three. Here, he took on assignments, gathered information and passed it on. Everyone knew he could be found here. The pub was crowded, mostly with City office workers who all stood around the bar. Paddy had not seen me enter. I bought him a double Jack Daniels, and myself a bourbon on the rocks. Might as well stay transatlantic. I set the glasses on the table and sat down in front of him.

"Hi Paddy."

He raised his watery eyes and regarded me. "Hello Jack." We were intimates.

I told him what I needed to know. He had heard about the murder at Beechurst.

"The man you want is Willy Kapowski. He's an engraver in Hatton Garden. Signet rings and stuff. He might not handle the merchandise himself, but he would give advice and send pros in the right direction."

Paddy wrote the address in a grimy notebook he took from his pocket. He tore the page and gave it to me.

"Only works there in the afternoons. Gets there about two."

I looked at the name. "Polish?"

"Was. Family fled from the Nazis before the war. Arrived here when he was about ten. Parents killed in the blitz."

"Ah. I like the Polish bit. Sounds quite promising."

I stayed with Paddy for another drink, then took a taxi back to the Morgan. I fed the meter. A fierce looking female parking warden was on the other side of the square, so I reckoned I was safe. I made my way on foot down the stretch of High Holborn to Hatton Garden, its shop front windows filled with gems and trinkets, testimony to its pre-eminence in the world of precious stones and metals. Eventually I found the right number. It was one of the older buildings. The board in the entrance showed Willy Kapowski on the third floor. I climbed narrow stairs.

The door to the Kapowski premises was locked, but there was a "please ring" notice under a bell. I pressed. A buzzer sounded within. The security arrangements were old-fashioned. The door had a small hatch in it which was pulled back, revealing two eyes and the bridge of a nose. The accent was cockney, not Polish.

"Yes, what is it?"

"I need a signet ring copied," I said.

There was a clatter of locks, and I found myself inside a small room, a workshop really, with a bench in front of a window. On it stood various small lathes and engraving tools. There was a powerful magnifying glass set on a moveable arm jutting from the wall and a flexible lamp which shone directly at the point of work.

Kapowski sat back in his chair and lifted one of his tools. He began to scratch away on a ring held firm in a vice. I sat down on a hard wooden chair which, apart from the safe, was the only other furniture in the room. Without looking up from his scratching Kapowski spoke first.

"Forget all this signet ring crap. What do you really want?"

"Information," I replied.

"You won't get that from me."

This was going to be tricky.

"Last Saturday there was a murder in a Sussex village. A wealthy young woman disturbed burglars in her house. They killed her but took away valuable jewels. Some of the pieces were quite old. They say you would be consulted about this merchandise."

"Who says?"

It was my turn to be difficult. "They do."

Kapowski stopped working and turned towards me. He studied me for a few moments. He was short and a touch overweight. He had a lot of nose and little chin. His hair, which was greasy, was smarmed tightly over his scalp. His eyes had that underpowered look which comes from working close up all the time.

"You're not a policeman. What are you? Some sort of private eye?"

I thought for a moment. The description was not flattering, but it was useful.

"Sort of," I replied.

"Well, you clearly don't know me," went on Kapowski. "If you did you'd know that even if I had the answers you wanted I would never give them to you!"

"The murder only happened on Saturday. You might not have been consulted yet. I'll call again in a day or two." I took a gamble. "The reason I'm interested is that I might want to buy the stuff."

Kapowski, who had returned to his work, shot me a glance. I had scored. I waited, but he said no more, so I got up to leave. As I reached the door he followed to let me out. I saw his hand move to an alarm switch which he turned off as he opened the door. I recognised the MicSec trademark.

"Come and see me again on Thursday," he said.

I went down the stairs encouraged.

Back at Lincoln's Inn Fields I found the Morgan clamped. The fierce parking warden was more observant than I thought. By the time the crew came to release the clamp and I had coughed up a fortune, I was hungry, so I decided on dinner at an Italian restaurant in Bayswater not far from the flat. I had gone there often in the past with Melissa and I half hoped she would be there. But she wasn't.

I was confident now that my theory that Martin was the murderer was correct. I reckoned he had already been in touch with Kapowski and would take the stuff to show him before Thursday. By the time I called it would be in the safe ready for inspection. Why Martin had murdered his wife was another question, but the question which now loomed above all others was the identity of the girl calling herself Davina, who had lured me to Beechurst. Why had she done it and where was she now? Was she working independently of Martin, or as his partner? Had she sent me on an errand of rescue or had I been lured into a trap? If so, why?

I ruminated over these things as I ate a rather sickly veal cordon bleu and downed it with a bottle of Frascati. I finished with zabaglione. I decided it would be wise after the alcohol to stay the night at the flat and drive to Beechurst in the morning. I used the payphone at the back of the restaurant to telephone Susan and tell her of my plans. I had warned her earlier in the day that I would not be requiring any meals, so she was not expecting me until late. Nevertheless, she sounded disappointed. In spite of the short period of our acquaintance, she was beginning to get used to my company.

Back at the flat, I turned on the late evening news. It was Melissa again. She looked very glamorous and her eyes sparkled. I wanted her badly. It was now seven months since I had arrived home at her flat to find my suitcase packed and standing in the hall. She had bought a rather smarter place than mine in Kensington and I lived there mostly. She was in the kitchen cooking. It was coque au vin. The table was laid with the best and the candles were already lit. As I came in, she took champagne from the fridge and poured two glasses.

"What are we celebrating?"

She laughed. "I'll tell you the second part later, but the first part is us."

She moved towards me, put her arms around my neck and gave me a deep amorous kiss. I forgot to ask about my luggage. We ate the meal in a tense, sexual atmosphere. We could not wait for coffee. Later in the bedroom when we lay drowsy and close, I remembered the second part of the celebrations and asked her what it was.

"You're leaving," was the simple reply.

At first I did not understand what she meant. Then I thought of the suitcase. Patiently, she explained. It was very Melissa.

"I think we should part for a while. There is something I need to find out about myself, but I don't want there to be any quarrels, and I want us to part on the highest possible note."

She had certainly achieved the high point.

"Is this forever?"

"No, I don't think so."

"How long?"

"Maybe six months, maybe six years."

I was not going to argue. It would become a row, and as she said, it was better to part on the high note. I dressed quickly. We kissed again in the hall. I picked up my bag and left. When I reached my own flat, the bed was cold and unwelcoming. I had not asked her whether there was somebody else, but somehow I didn't think there was.

About a week later I realised that she had forgotten to pack my cuff-links, so I returned one afternoon and rang the bell. It was answered by a young girl, very beautiful, in her early twenties. I thought that she was a model, but in fact, she did Melissa's make-up at the studio. Melissa was out, but I explained what I wanted. She let me in and I went to the bedroom. The cuff-links were on the silver dish on the dressing table where Melissa kept her earrings. I noticed the bed was rumpled. There was underwear and clothes about the room, all female. Some things were Melissa's but some were not. The girl was standing in the doorway. I looked at her. She looked at me.

"Melissa doesn't want you to know."

I stared at the cuff-links in my palm.

"I had better leave these here then," I said, dropping them back in the dish.

The girl nodded. She was clearly nervous as she saw me to the door.

"Don't worry," I called over my shoulder, 'Your grubby secret is safe with me!'

Instantly I felt mean. I turned to say sorry, but she quickly closed the door.

As I reached the street my confusion gave way to a sense of hurt. I was not jealous. Indeed, from that point of view, it was easier that Melissa's lover was a girl, but I was upset that she had not confided in me. Surely Melissa above all others should have had faith in my attitude of live and let live.

A disturbing voice told me that this was because she had detected that my hostility to the establishment was tinged with that degree of respect, comfort even, which caused me to operate on its fringes, but not completely outside its borders. A respect which kept me in an office in the attics of *Whilloes* rather than on my own in an alley off Fleet Street, and sent me scurrying home to Messamer Hall for Christmas.

Melissa acknowledged my Oxfam jacket, but noticed also the handmade shoes. Perhaps she saw confusing signals which reduced her confidence in my ability to accept her experiment in a gay relationship.

I tried to beat the traffic by setting off early the following morning, but the only way to do that these days in the South is to travel in the middle of the night. The only comfort as I struggled out of London at a crawl was that the incoming traffic was crawling even slower. I was impatient, because after my success with Kapowski I had another idea to pursue. I wanted somebody to tell me about the old times at The Grange, and I reckoned Elderflower's daughter, Rosa, would be the one to approach.

I reached that monument to architectural ugliness shortly before eleven. There was a special path at the side for tradesmen to prevent the passage of such vulgar folk spoiling the dignity of the main drive, and I took it to the back door which was down a flight of steps in a basement area. I was in luck. It was Rosa who answered my knock. She was much as I had imagined. Plump, fresh faced, with high cheek bones, and hair, perhaps a little greyer than I expected, drawn back tight into a bun. The white apron rose over her ample bosom. I offered my hand.

"St John Whilloe. I just thought I would call and congratulate you on that splendid dinner you cooked on Saturday night in what must have been very trying circumstances!"

She smiled nervously, revealing chinks of gold from a rather battered row of teeth. She rubbed her hands on her apron before clasping mine with a firmness which was reassuring. I stood for a moment.

"Are you going to ask me in?"

She was momentarily confused. "Well, of course, yes. I'm not used to Mr Michener's guests calling like this to offer their thanks. Why," she laughed, "it has never happened before. Come in and I will make you some coffee."

As she clattered about the kitchen, making strong mocha coffee in a cafetiere, I admired the surroundings. Unlike the rest of the property, this part of it, although old-fashioned, was very homely. The kitchen was a big room, as big, I thought, as the dining room upstairs. In the centre was a huge scrubbed deal table at which I sat, and all around were dressers and shelves filled with china, glass and cooking utensils, many of which hung, handy and ready for use, at just the point at which they would be needed. At one end of the table was the paraphernalia of pastry making, upon which Rosa had been about to embark when I called. A large saucepan gave off a delicious smell of herbs and stock as it simmered gently on a great red Aga, which contributed to the cosy, safe atmosphere.

Rosa poured me coffee, black and steaming in a plain white cup of the kind you find in France at breakfast. I sipped and savoured.

At length I said reflectively, "It must have been awful having Mrs Michener, your mistress, murdered."

Rosa regarded me steadily. She looked as if she was about to say something profound, but after an interval all she said was, "Yes, it was."

I detected that loyalty had intervened. I was an outsider after all. This was an establishment where there must be a strong insider bond. Refugees arriving from Hitler before the war and making their way in a foreign land, master and servants staying together. Rosa's husband fleeing the Russian crackdown in Hungary to find sanctuary and a wife. These people would certainly guard each other's secrets and would not be readily tempted into betrayal. I decided to try fishing deeper and cast my line.

"Did you work here, Rosa, when Mr Martin Michener was a child?"

Her eyes brightened, and she spoke, smiling. "Oh yes. He was born here. In those days, my mother was the cook and housekeeper, and I helped with everything."

"Did you enjoy that?"

"In a manner of speaking yes, but the, how shall I say, atmosphere was not good."

"How do you mean?"

Another hesitation. The loyalty obstacle. I was patient. At length Rosa replied.

"Things were not easy in the family at that time. Eva, old Mrs Michener had died, and Mr Michener had married a girl so much younger. It was such a change, and we felt... well, we felt it showed a lack of respect for Eva, who had done so much for us. Then, Mr Arnold came to live here with Katherine. So there were two young Mrs Micheners in the house at once. Both became pregnant. It didn't seem right somehow."

Rosa fell silent again.

"Was there anything else?"

"Well, you have probably heard. I don't know why Dorothy married old Stanley. She cannot have been happy. When she became pregnant he accused her of having an affair with Titus Mynot. Dorothy left and that was that. When Katherine had her baby it was refreshing to have a new life to distract us."

It did all sound rather dramatic, especially after the trials the family had been through, having to leave Poland and so on. I hoped my sympathy would encourage her. She moved off the subject slightly.

"I remember that later old Stanley was besotted with his grandson. He used to sit with him on his knee for hours. Because of his illness, the old man had to have an afternoon nap. Sometimes I used to put the little mite on the bed beside him so that he could have his rest as well. Stanley loved this. I think it was his fascination with the child that kept him going towards the end."

Rosa filled my coffee cup. As she was doing so, she murmured almost to herself, "It was so strange when he died."

I pressed her to explain. There was more hesitation before Rosa told me that one afternoon she had followed the usual practice of putting the little boy on the bed beside old Stanley. It was king size, so there was no danger of the baby rolling off. When she came to wake them, the old man had died.

"It was so strange," she repeated, "because the little baby's personality then changed. In a curious way, from that moment, although he was still a baby, he became... well, he became like old Stanley."

This was curious. Spooky even. I began to wonder.

"How old was the baby then?"

"Just six months old," replied Rosa.

Now, it was my turn to fall silent. Maybe there was an explanation for Martin's peculiar aura. I was beginning to catch a glimpse of something which most rational people would say could not have happened.

Presently Rosa spoke again. "You know, Mr Whilloe, I have never said this to anyone before, but it was as if the baby had died and the old man lived on in the child. It was really odd. Sometimes I used to worry that I was mad."

She began to look anxiously at the clock, and I could see it was time to go. I thanked her for the coffee. She told me to call again. I promised I would, and I meant it. I was sure she had more to tell.

CHAPTER FIVE

I was thoughtful as I made my way back to Briar Cottage. Rosa was saying the baby took on the aspect of the old man after Stanley died. Could such a swap occur? Surely not? Yet one read and saw on television children who remembered past lives, who knew details about events which happened before they were born. Orthodox science dismissed these things but they happened nevertheless.

I had never been one to dwell on the paranormal but I was attracted to it, largely because scientific correctness said it could not be. I liked anything which had been rejected by any sort of prejudice. If Martin had acquired an aspect of old Stanley, even if only in his imagination, might he not be following some secret plan to avenge the old man's rejection by his young wife? It sounded pretty stupid as I thought about it, but I felt I had to find out more. But from whom? Perhaps there was a book?

That afternoon I would go to the library in Chichester, but first I needed to make a phone call. I carried the number of the public phone of the Iron Duke just in case. It was answered by one of the office workers, happily boozing away a generous lunch hour, who fetched Paddy from his alcove. I asked him to trace the circumstances of the life and death of Dorothy Skillette, believed to have died of a stroke near Lincoln a couple of years ago. I arranged to meet up with him on Thursday, before going to my second visit with Kapowski.

In the library I thumbed through books of the paranormal, but it was all a bit far-fetched, and I was not quite sure what I was looking for. I found a list of professional bodies and associations to which people who dabbled in these things belonged. I eventually rang the Society of Hypnotherapists. The girl there was very helpful. She appeared to understand what I was talking about and recommended I contact a retired professor of psychology from one of the Oxford colleges, who now lived in North Treford in the Cotswolds. A certain Jefferson Tewkesbury, who having completed his life as an academic, started a fresh career as a hypnotherapist. His speciality was regressing people into supposed previous lives. He had written and broadcast on his subject and was widely respected by people interested in this field. I found his number in the phone book without difficulty. He was attentive as I briefly explained my interest and agreed to see me the very next day.

Back in my room in Briar Cottage I studied my notes. I suspected that the source of the mystery lay at the time of the affair between Stanley's young wife and Titus Mynot, but that did not explain why Martin had killed his wife. It certainly did not explain the visit to my office of the mysterious girl. Nor did it explain the strange note that I received from the real Davina Mynot with the invitation to meet her in the dark in the churchyard. It would have made some sense if the two Davina's were the same, but not as they were different. Had Davina lived, she would have entertained me to dinner on an invitation issued by her impostor. This I found the most confusing aspect of the whole mystery. Were the two Davina's working together in some way? I had the feeling I was finding too many new questions and too few real answers.

Later on downstairs, I found my landlady radiant in a new hairdo and what looked as if they were new clothes. They were, anyway, younger, fresher and less stuffy than the twin set and tweeds. A crisp denim shirt worn over a salmon pink cotton polo neck gave an interesting line to well-shaped breasts. The navy twill skirt was calf length and full, and a new pair of long boots of the best quality brown leather gave her an altogether more dramatic aspect. As she moved around I caught the hint of expensive scent.

I wondered if all this had been done for me. She had been widowed for some time, after all, but I was sure I was too bohemian a character to attract somebody of Susan's predictable background. Anyway, with Melissa constantly on my mind, and the very attractive bogus Davina apparently somewhere alive and well, I felt I had no need of yet another woman to complicate my life. Susan was not the type to be on for sex without emotional complications. Having reached this decision, it was annoying to hear my voice suggesting that perhaps it would be nice to visit the pub after dinner. It was all the more annoying when she replied that yes, it would be very nice indeed.

The Crown was only a few hundred yards from Briar Cottage. Quaint with low beams, but with an aspect of continually refurbished antiqueness which is common to so many of these old pubs nowadays. Nevertheless, it was warm and cosy, offered a good selection of real ales and was not very busy. No doubt at the weekends it would be jammed.

We had left Jennifer safe at the cottage, finishing her homework. Susan and I sat at a table near the fire. She surprised me by drinking locally brewed ale, so I joined her. I took great gulps. It tasted good. Susan let me lead the conversation. She was clearly anxious to please. I asked her about her husband. It turned out they had been married for five years, and Craig, that was his name, had been a geological engineer working on an oil rig. I remembered the explosion. Many lives had been lost. At the time Susan and her husband had been living in Scotland, near Aberdeen. Financially things worked out because he had plenty of life assurance, and the company paid substantial compensation.

Susan was born at Briar Cottage and brought up in the village. Later, after Craig's death, her father retired and her parents moved to Cornwall. They put forward the idea of Susan moving into her old home with Jennifer. It made sense to be in familiar surroundings among old friends. The idea was a success, and they had been happy.

Discovering that Susan had been brought up in Beechurst was something of a bonus. I tried not to press her for information, but I could not help it. Anyway, I was on assignment and had a job to do. She filled in some gaps. Dorothy Skillette, Stanley's second wife, came from a wealthy family not unlike the Mynots, farms and so on. They were appalled when she decided to marry the old Pole, who was old enough to be her grandfather. Money did not interest them because they already had plenty. They virtually cut her off. After Stanley banished her she went back to Lincoln and lived somewhere in a cottage. She had not kept the baby, but Susan was not sure whether she had had an abortion or whether it was adopted. Adoption was more likely as abortion was not legal in those days.

I asked about Arnold and Katherine. Their marriage seemed quite happy, but Arnold had a reputation for being a philanderer, although Susan conceded that this might have been wishful thinking. I enquired about Katherine's death, which was at the relatively young age of 63, but there was nothing mysterious about this. Cancer. She had smoked like a chimney and refused all advice to cut down or give up.

Martin was known to be very clever and went straight into the business after gaining an engineering degree at Loughborough. He was the drive and brains behind the expansion of the security division, which had been started by Arnold.

I wanted to know more about the real Davina, but I had to be careful because I was supposed to know her, so I fished gingerly. All I gained was a picture of a very horsy person, permanently dressed in a waxed coat and green wellies. I asked Susan how such a girl had coped with The Grange. On the surface with good humour, dismissing the whole peculiar set-up as rather fun, describing Elderflower as an *absolute sweetheart* and Rosa as a *perfect cook*. But Susan detected some strain behind the public persona. Davina often returned to her parents' farm. She kept her horses there. I remarked on the absence of children, but according to Susan, Martin was hardly ever at home. The head office of the Company was in London, and the family still retained Arnold's old flat as a pied-à-terre in the capital, whilst the factory was near Manchester. So business commitments kept him away a great deal.

Having fished a useful catch, I refilled the glasses and felt an obligation to let the conversation drift to a more social level. Susan asked about my novel. I was unprepared, having forgotten all about it, and made vague excuses about getting in the mood to get started. She was surprisingly direct and asked if I had a girlfriend. I told her about Melissa, although I did not actually identify her, and I did not give the details of the break-up, just that it had happened. I was surprised that Susan had not married again. I asked her a rather silly question about what she missed the most in widowhood. It must have been the beer talking.

Her reply was again direct. "Having a man."

She left no doubt that she did not mean putting up shelves. I blushed and gulped my beer. Somehow I had never got over the uncomfortable aspect of relationships between the sexes, stemming from the monastic life of a single sex public school, with its undertone of abuse.

Later, after we had walked back to the cottage arm in arm, Susan suggested coffee. I waited on the sofa in the sitting room, wondering what was to happen next. I had clearly misjudged this woman. When we first met I thought she was neat and prim and very reserved, and if she had any interest in men at all, they would be of the conventional kind. My shaggy beard and corduroy jacket would turn her from my direction. Instead, these defences seemed to have beckoned her forward.

Susan came into the lounge with a tray, which she set on the low table in front of me and sat down on the sofa, close. I could smell her perfume and sense her softness, as her hand, probably on purpose, brushed my knee as she arranged the cups. When she had poured she turned to face me. Her eyes sparkling, her cheeks lightly flushed, her lips moist and slightly parted. I knew she wanted to be kissed. For a moment I hesitated, then went for it. There had been no one since Melissa after all.

We kissed long and deep. Whenever we parted Susan whispered "Oh God" and pulled my head towards her again. Eventually we had to break away to breathe. I had all but lost my common sense, and out of politeness rather than conviction, I said "What about Jenny?"

Susan sighed. She straightened her rumpled clothes and sipped coffee.

"St John..."

I interjected. "You can call me Jack."

"Jack? That's horrid. St John is a lovely name. Jenny is going away at the weekend. She will be away Friday and Saturday, back on Sunday afternoon. Let's wait until then."

I moved across to the fireplace and stood looking down at her. I knew what I wanted to say, but I was not sure I could say it in the right way. As I looked at her I ran it through my mind. It went like this:

Susan, I think this may be a mistake. I am a very involved sort of person. I am sort of committed elsewhere. Of course, I find you attractive and exciting, but you have had sadness in your life, and I would hate to think of your being hurt again, particularly if I were the cause of it.

It sounded in my head like prissy crap so I said nothing. Susan got up from the sofa and stood very close to me. Friday would be a long wait.

CHAPTER SIX

North Treford is a large village typical of the Cotswolds, reassuring in its cloak of aged and well-dressed stone. The winding main street opens out into a cosy square with a friendly mixture of houses and shops. In the centre of the green a great sycamore raises its domed crown to a height of over a hundred feet. Around the base of the tree a circular wooden seat has been built, so that the people of the village, or more commonly nowadays, tourists, can sit and pass the time of day.

Like all Cotswold villages, this one is on the tourist map, but there are few obvious signs of this. There is a car park just off the square, and public lavatories built to resemble a small house. The two inns have been expanded to offer en suite accommodation and undoubtedly receive more visitors than would be the case if they were not on the track beaten by itinerant Americans and Japanese. At one time, the main street formed a part of the trunk road to Cheltenham, but through traffic is now carried along a bypass about a mile to the north.

Professor Tewkesbury lives in one of the houses on the square, next door but one to the post office. The frontage is narrow, but the property has great depth, as I discovered when a tall, ascetic man with neat grey hair and goatee beard greeted my knock. He led me through a dim passage, which twice dropped down steps before we reached his study overlooking the garden.

This was a charming room with an inglenook fire, low beams, stone flagged floor and walls covered by white painted shelves full of books. Against one wall stood a table with a word processor, very up to date, and papers stacked high. A leather swivel chair, circular and probably Victorian, stood in front of the table. Beside the fireplace a large easy chair, covered in chintz to match the curtains and piled with cushions, looked inviting as the professor waved me to it. The professor sat himself by the table and swivelled the chair towards me.

"I thought it would be best if we talked together first, and then we will join my wife, Hjørdis, for tea in the sitting room."

Hjørdis? Scandinavian. Finnish probably. Tewkesbury was too aesthetic to satisfy a rapacious Swede.

He leant forward solicitously. "Are you comfortable?"

"Very much so. I could almost fall asleep in this!" I responded with a laugh.

"Ah," nodded the professor, "quite right. My clients sit there when they are under hypnosis. This room really isn't big enough for a couch."

The cushions were covered with heavy woollen covers woven in dramatic Nordic designs. Professor Tewkesbury detected my interest.

"Hjørdis is a weaver. She has a studio at the top of the house and specialises in items for furnishing. Cushion covers, wall hangings, rugs and so on."

I studied the professor as he spoke. His eyes were clear blue and rather intense. He wore a matching blue roll neck under a soft tweed jacket. Twill trousers with a knife edge press accentuated his long legs, but an academic aspect was added to his neat appearance by his small, well trimmed beard. I liked him immediately and felt confident he knew his subject.

"Professor Tewkesbury," I began, "this is a complicated and rather strange story."

"In that case, Mr Whilloe, it is best that you lean back, relax completely and tell me, in your own words, from the very beginning."

I did just that. I began with the fake Davina's visit to my office and finished with my conversation with Rosa the day before. I laid emphasis on the creepy atmosphere of The Grange, and the disturbance I felt when in Martin's company. I repeated Martin's strange phrase from the night of the dinner, and of course, faithfully recalled all the details Rosa had described of Stanley's death and its apparent effect on the baby.

Professor Tewkesbury listened intently and let me finish without a single interruption. He took notes on a pad resting on his knee. Occasionally he nodded his head, and at other times shook it. He seemed to have no difficulty in following the narrative. When I had finished, he was silent for a while. Stroking his beard with the tip of his left forefinger the professor stared at me thoughtfully. His cheeks were gaunt and his brow deep.

Suddenly he refocused his blue eyes. I think he had been looking through me rather than at me.

"What do you know of things we call paranormal?"

"Nothing."

"Have you ever had a paranormal experience?"

Had I? Apart from these weird vibes at The Grange I certainly had not.

"No."

The professor paused. He talked with a correct rather than refined accent and chose his words carefully. Once he began speaking he kept going as if from a memorised text. A habit left over, I surmised, from his years as a don.

"That's good. I shall not have to waste time persuading you to change your ideas. A clean, fresh mind!" He smiled. "There are many things that science has yet to find answers for in the material world, which in recent centuries has always taken priority over the spiritual or metaphysical aspect of life. There is even evidence that primitive peoples in the past may have had a greater spiritual consciousness than we have today. Call it instinct to make it sound more familiar."

I nodded. Having selected his words Tewkesbury continued.

"No one knows for sure whether such phenomena as regression to previous lives, the ability to foretell events, spiritual healing, communication with the dead and such things as these are actual or imagined. Whether they do actually happen or whether they are some form of projection from the consciousness, or perhaps inherited memory, is far from certain. What I have tried to do in my own small way is to concentrate on phenomena where *I* have evidence of something, which I can then explore with confidence that the manifestation, if not the actual happening, is at least a reality. Are you with me?"

I nodded again.

"Good. Therefore I can rely on you to be rational and understand that what we are talking about in your case is only a supposition, a theory perhaps, but certainly not a proven fact?"

A lot of health warnings here. Nevertheless I was not deterred. "You can rely on that."

Tewkesbury stretched his long legs.

"Well done. Let me explain. Some people believe that it is possible that a soul in an old body with unfinished work and determined to live on, can, if in proximity to the very young soul of an infant, effect an exchange, so that it is the infant's soul which passes to eternity in the old body and the old soul which lives on in the infant. The theory was developed by an American, a Professor of Paranormal Studies at one of the Californian universities. The Americans are more courageous when exploring the frontiers of our perceptions. They are less fearful of ridicule. Their research is driven by possibilities, whereas ours is restrained by impossibilities.

"Professor Weintraut asserts that all children are born innocent with a cleansed, if not new, soul. If they subsequently become evil or demented, it is because their psyche has been inhabited by a spirit which has left the path of enlightenment. Without passing into the hereafter on the death of its body, the dark spirit moves forcefully to inhabit the body of a young child, casting out the infant soul in the process. The theory fits quite well with ancient beliefs regarding derangement, which was thought to be evidence of possession by the devil. Weintraut calls it *Aggressive Spiritual Exchange*."

I suppose I expected the professor to say something like this. It was what I had come to the Cotswolds to hear, yet having heard it, it sounded unreal, absurd even. The stuff of late night movies, but not of real life.

"Professor, do *you* believe in this sort of thing?"

Tewkesbury regarded me earnestly. "As I have suggested already I try to avoid the concept of belief. As I think you know, I have become interested in these things since my retirement. I practise hypnotherapy which has given me an insight into a great deal. I have not actually encountered a case of *this* sort, so I am without evidence upon which I can rely."

At this point, Tewkesbury stood up and walked to the window. He stared out into the garden for some time before returning to his chair.

"One of the problems of studying subjects of this kind is that it is the intellectual equivalent of eating a meringue. The substance seems to melt away just as you get to grips with it. There is something there, but before you can make sure, it is gone. And then, of course, there are crackpots, who over dramatise everything and cause a lot of confusion."

I asked him what he thought of the Michener case. He replied that as I had described it, if such a thing were possible, then this could be genuine. He looked at me earnestly once again.

"You must understand, that for it to work, the old soul must have a very compelling reason to exchange. Here, it seems, a violent and acute hate developed not only against the young wife, but against her child, which you told me could not have been his. The purpose of living in the baby would be to grow up as more or less the same age as that other child."

I asked the professor why, if Martin was really his grandfather still living, he should have killed his wife. The professor did not reply at once. He studied his notes for a moment.

"Let me try and explain the outcome of this concept of Aggressive Spiritual Exchange. We are not dealing with a simple process of an old man walking around in a young body. All the scientifically identifiable elements of the body are still the original, as are the genes. If the soul changes, and remember, although it is the basis of religious faith, there is absolutely no scientific proof of the existence of the soul, it would have to manipulate the inhabited psyche. So it would be like the sub-conscious Stanley setting Martin up into situations which would force the conscious Martin to act to carry out the sub-conscious Stanley's will."

"You mean like schizophrenia?"

"Somewhat, but not quite. With schizophrenia you have what is in effect a split consciousness. In this case, you have a consciousness which is one person, and a sub-conscious which is a completely different person, inhabiting the same body."

"When I talk to Martin, am I really talking to Stanley?"

"No, you are talking to Martin, but Stanley is listening in."

"Does Stanley ever talk?"

"Not in the conscious sense, but he influences what Martin says."

I thought for a moment. "Could Stanley ever take over completely so that Martin's personality receded, disappeared even?"

The professor hesitated. "We are dealing with something which may not be real, which is beyond scientific proof and is probably beyond the frontiers of our understanding anyway. However, yes, I think such a thing could happen, but only in an extreme situation."

He paused. This was very taxing stuff, but I felt I was following the drift of the professor's explanation.

"I think I can cope with that, but how does it explain Martin murdering his wife?"

"Well," said the professor, "if everything is as you have described, the normal Martin would seek to heal the feud between the families. He falls in love with, then marries, Titus's niece. The sub-conscious Stanley encourages this in order to bring the girl within his grasp. Next, Stanley would need to cause an event which would in turn cause Martin to kill his wife, an event which Martin would remember in the same way he would remember a scene of a film, but would have no remorse because his sub-consciousness was responsible for initiating the act."

This fitted the strange detachment that I had encountered when I had dinner with Martin on the night of the murder.

The professor consulted his notes once more, then continued. "I think we know why Stanley organised the killing of Davina. It is part of his vengeance. We do not yet know why Martin actually killed her. There will be a real and tangible reason for this."

"And the fake Davina?" I asked. "What of her?"

"I am afraid I cannot see that. There is a web of intrigue here which is yet to be unravelled. I fancy that this girl who pretended to be Davina has more to do with Martin than with old Stanley. You must remember that Martin is most likely an intriguer in his own right. You must assume that he is rationally motivated, even wicked. The Stanley option should be held in reserve. One thing is certain, however, and of this you must take heed."

I looked at him. "What is that?"

"If the Stanley option is valid, in other words, if the exchange of his soul to the baby did happen, his target is Dorothy's baby. Now grown up and about his own age. We do not know whether the baby is male or female, and we cannot be sure that the person is still alive, but if he or she is, that person is Stanley's target. He has already killed twice, so we can be sure that that person is now in mortal danger."

"Killed twice?" I was not clear what the professor was saying.

"Yes. Davina recently, but earlier the baby Martin. If this theory is at all valid, it would be the baby who was forced to die in old Stanley's body. The key word is *forced*. It would not have been voluntary."

A tingle ran up my spine.

The professor continued. "Mr Whilloe, I think you must make it your business to find that person before he or she is found by Martin Michener."

I heard the sound of crockery. Tewkesbury stood up beaming.

"Ah," he said, "Hjørdis is preparing tea. Let us go through to the sitting room."

I followed him back along the passage and up two steps, then through a doorway into a cosy room which looked out onto the square. Larger than the one we had left, but of the same style, with a similar inglenook fireplace in which a bright log fire burned. There were one or two bookshelves, but in this room the walls were almost entirely covered with woven tapestries as if in a hall of a miniature medieval castle. I could detect a relationship in the designs, though the materials varied. Some were exquisitely delicate and thin, others were robust with lumpy surfaces, reminding me of great wraps to keep the arctic chill at bay.

"I take it these are all Mrs Tewkesbury's designs?"

The professor nodded. "Every one."

At that moment Hjørdis entered the room carrying a tray. She was strikingly tall, nearly six foot in flat shoes, accentuated by the straightness of her body, which was feminine yet lean. Her blond hair was fading grey here and there, and her open face had the characteristically Scandinavian high cheek bones. She wore a wool dress which was long to mid-calf, adding dignity and force to her height. Odd bits of Celtic style jewellery hinted at her artistic talent, but the overall impression, even in her late fifties, was of glamour with a bohemian touch. Yet the line of her mouth was hard and the glint in her eye determined. She struck me as one used to having her own way.

The professor introduced us formally. "Hjørdis, this is Mr Whilloe. Mr Whilloe, this is Hjørdis Foss, one of Europe's great artistic weavers!"

Foss? She does not use her husband's name? Just as I thought. Her own woman. We sat down. I was given a cup of tea. Leaf tea poured through an exquisite silver strainer worked with blue enamel. I had assumed Hjørdis to be Finnish. When I let this slip in early conversation, I was corrected with a curt announcement that she was Norwegian, accompanied by a withering look. I ate two pieces of cake to make amends.

The conversation stayed well clear of aggressive spiritual exchange. I had the impression that whilst the professor took a great interest in his wife's weaving, she was less interested in his hypnotherapy. Although the hint of bohemian tolerance in her appearance suggested a flexibility of mind, I suspected that her attitudes were pretty rigid. Paranormal theories would not appeal. Thus the conversation centred upon her artistic efforts, and as it did so, I began to see that weaving a tapestry was the mirror image of unravelling a mystery. The weaver took the yarns and interlocked them into a pattern in which the individual strands could not be recognised by the untutored eye. Likewise, a mystery was an event, or set of events, forming a pattern which concealed the reality of the individual parts. Once the individual parts could be identified, the mystery would unravel.

At length, it was time to go. I thanked Hjørdis for the tea. She beamed and presented a cheek for a kiss. Maybe she liked me, in spite of my interest in her husband's grasp of the unreal. The professor escorted me to the door. He shook my hand warmly.

"Good luck with your mission. Remember that on one level you are at the outer edge of human understanding, but that on another, you are confronting basic wickedness. Take care!"

I nodded. "May I call upon you again for advice if needed?"

"Of course, dear boy. At any time."

Outside it was quite dark and the air was chill. I broke my usual habit and put the Morgan's hood up before setting off. I took the minor roads to avoid the conurbations. These would now be spewing their working populations into rivers of traffic which would fill the main roads and motorways.

I was pleased with my visit to the professor. He and his wife were an interesting couple in any event, but the professor's theories had provided me with a stimulating thought process upon which to build my enquiries. Irrational certainly, but with that peculiar edge of the spooky to which many sane people have found themselves drawn.

Taken literally, the concept of aggressive spiritual exchange could form a theory of what motivated Martin Michener and could even provide an explanation, rather than a motive, for the killing of his wife. Nevertheless I found it hard, no, I think impossible, to accept. I preferred a simplified version which suggested Martin was unbalanced, perhaps even believing he was some sort of reincarnation of his grandfather, and that this distorted self-awareness governed some aspects of his life. It was all a baffling tangle and the only way forward was to pull at the threads until the mystery began to unravel.

Tomorrow I was to see Paddy again, and I hoped he would give me more information about Dorothy Skillette. In the afternoon I had another meeting arranged with Willy Kapowski. He might show me some of the jewels, but having not seen them before, they would be unlikely to offer me any clues. Somehow, I would have to get Willy to admit that it was Martin who had brought them to him. Remembering the professor's warning, it was urgent that I now search for clues which would lead me to the identity of Dorothy Skillette's child. I was sure that once I knew the identity of that person I would be close to knowing everything.

I reached Briar Cottage just in time for dinner. Susan seemed radiant, whilst Jennifer chatted happily about her weekend trip. I thought of our weekend assignation with anticipation. Once or twice I caught Susan's eye.

CHAPTER SEVEN

Paddy Flynn was waiting for me in his usual corner seat at the Iron Duke. He looked pleased with himself. I was hungry, so I ordered two plates of bangers and mash. While we tucked in, Paddy recounted minor adventures during his researches over the last two days, which were not interesting enough to record, but which I listened to because he expected it.

When we were on the second round of drinks he began to feed out the information I wanted to hear. Most of what I had picked up in the village seemed to be correct. Dorothy Skillette's family had been none too pleased when she decided to go to London to work as a secretary, and they had indeed cut her off completely when she married old Stanley. When in turn he threw her out, and she went back to Lincoln pregnant, they considered it very bad news indeed. The girl had some resources of her own, apparently, having benefited from a trust fund, and she had to make do with these. They allowed her to rent one of their estate cottages, and there she had continued to live.

"What about the baby?" I asked.

"It was adopted."

"Was it a boy or a girl?"

"Nobody seems to know. It was all very secretive in a nursing home in London."

"Did you enquire?"

"Closed down years ago."

"Oh." That was a disappointment. I switched tack. "Did she die of a stroke?"

"She had a stroke, but she didn't die. She is still alive."

For a moment I thought I had the key to the whole mystery. Surely Dorothy Skillette would tell me all that I needed to know once I explained the importance, but it turned out that while she had survived, she was substantially paralysed and unable to speak, living in a private home for incurables on the outskirts of Lincoln itself. Nevertheless, it would be worth a visit. I congratulated Paddy on his efforts, yet I felt he was hiding something up his sleeve. I bought another round of drinks. Orange juice for me this time. A thought struck me.

"Is it a private home?"

"Yes, and very expensive."

"Did you find out who pays the fees for her?"

"Yes, I did," said Paddy.

I began to sense something. I leant forward impatiently. "For Christ's sake, Paddy, stop pissing around! Who pays the fees?"

"*Whilloes.*"

I was dumbfounded. "What do you mean, '*Whilloes*'?"

"They pay her fees monthly."

I could not believe it. "Are you sure of this, Paddy?"

"Quite sure."

"Whose money are they using to pay? Hers or somebody else's?"

Paddy laughed. When he did this his face grew redder.

"I should have thought you could find that out for yourself. It's your family firm after all!"

I could think of nothing to say. Paddy went to the bar and returned with a bourbon on the rocks for me.

"Orange juice is no good for shocks."

My mind returned to my quizzing of Gerard about the fake Davina's visit. He had specifically said that the firm did not act for the Micheners, but neither of us had mentioned the Skillettes, nor, of course, the Mynots. It was possible there had been a change of heart. After the public row could there have been something of a reconciliation? When Martin married Davina, had she persuaded her Uncle Titus to cough up to support the old lady in her illness? It would not be easy to wring this information out of Gerard. He was a stickler for confidentiality and legal etiquette.

I looked at my watch. It was a quarter to three. Time to move on to Hatton Garden. I took a brown envelope full of bank notes and slipped it across to Paddy.

"What about expenses?" he asked.

"They're included in there."

"How do you know how much they were?"

"There's enough," I said firmly.

The Irishman took the envelope and slipped it into his jacket.

I stood up and put a hand on his shoulder. "Watch the drink, old friend, this assignment is not over yet."

This time I had parked the Morgan in a public car park. Costly though this was, it was cheaper than the clamps. The afternoon was gloomy now and a fine rain carried by a strong wind rushed towards me as I made my way down the street. I was glad of the stockman's coat and turned up the collar.

After the usual peeping ritual through the hatch in the door, Kapowski let me in to his little workshop. This time, laid out on the work bench, was a piece of black velvet. The flexible lamp had been turned to shine directly onto various pieces of jewellery set out for my inspection. There was a pearl and ruby brooch, a diamond square brooch, a diamond necklace and a pair of delightful sapphire earrings with a ring to match.

"Is this all?" I asked.

"All that is available."

"All that is available, or all that is available to me?"

"To you."

I know nothing about jewellery, but I picked up one or two pieces and admired them. I suspected I was looking at items designed and made in the nineteen thirties.

"This is all pre-war, isn't it?"

Kapowski nodded.

"How much?"

"Three K."

This was clearly cheap when compared with retail values, but I suspected on the high side for stolen property.

"I'll think about it."

Kapowski nodded and began to roll up the black velvet.

"Did Martin Michener bring them himself?"

Kapowski smiled and slipped the roll into the safe. He twisted the combination. It was a new safe bearing the MicSec trademark.

"I need to be sure the stuff is genuine," I ventured.

"You have my word it is."

The only way to get this man to talk was to get heavy. "Kapowski, I need this information."

"I told you. I don't give information."

"You have the merchandise. There has been a murder. Some friends at Scotland Yard may like to ask you some questions."

A look of resignation crossed his brow, almost as if he expected me to say this, but he shook his head and returned to his workbench. He adjusted the light to shine on the vice, in which a ring, different to last time, was clamped and began working. I was uncertain what to do next. Seizing him by the throat and hurling him against the wall may be the next step in a TV drama, but I was not sure I could do it. I would have to think of something else.

"Think it over. I'll come back and see you in a couple of hours."

Kapowski turned from his light. The side of his face was brightly illuminated. His greasy hair gleamed and his oily skin had little droplets of sweat, but his eyes blazed defiance.

"I know who you are. You're the dirty tricks man from a posh firm of solicitors. You can come back in two hours, two days, two weeks, two months or two years, but I will never, never give you the information you want!"

With that, Kapowski moved to the door, opened it and stood waiting for me to leave. Feeling stupid in defeat, I meekly made my way to the street. Disappointment leaves a bitter taste. I found a café and, after collecting a mug of hot water with a tea bag floating in it at the counter, made myself comfortable at a plastic table in the corner.

"Milk and sugar is on the table," explained the girl. She was cheerful enough, but like the establishment, a little the worse for wear.

As I waited for something that looked drinkable to brew, I added the new pieces to the jigsaw. Dorothy Skillette was alive and her fees were paid by *Whilloes*, yet my plan to extract a confession of Martin Michener's identity from Kapowski had, after early promise, failed. I was still no nearer proving that he had murdered his wife, nor who the mysterious girl was, nor why she had come to see me in the first place. I stirred my so-called tea.

Maybe the professor was right. Perhaps Martin and this unknown girl were working together, but if so, to what end? What was the amazing discovery that the real Davina had made which caused her to deliver the note inviting me to meet her at the churchyard? Why meet there? Was this knowledge the cause of her murder? My invitation to The Grange for dinner had originally been extended by the fake Davina, yet from the note and Martin's telephone call, it was clear that both he and the real Davina were expecting me. Were they all working together for some reason? Oddly enough, the only part of this strange affair which made any sense at all was the professor's theory of aggressive spiritual exchange, yet this ought to have been beyond belief. All the other facts and incidents appeared both contradictory and confusing.

There was some good news. I could visit Dorothy Skillette, although it would not help much because she was paralysed and comatose. What was this business of the fees? Why were *Whilloes* paying? What was the connection? Why had Gerard not taken me into his confidence?

As I continued to sit in the greasy café thinking over these things, I began to feel curiously alone. It was now a week since a girl of whom I had never heard before, who turned out not to be who she said she was, had walked into my life, persuading me to become involved in a story of lies, violence, deception and jealousy, which had already claimed one life, and which according to the professor, threatened to claim another whose identity as yet we did not know.

What disturbed me was not just the web in which I, too, was now entangled, but the shock to my sense of purpose. I was a rebel, but I was rebelling against well established rules and values. The way I led my own life was to cock a snook at other people's, yet I was cocking a snook at privileged lives which obeyed the rules of which I did not approve. Now I was coming into close contact with different sorts of lives, run much more according to the rules made up by the individual people who led them to suit themselves. I was close to people less concerned about what others would think than they were in how they themselves felt. The Micheners in their crazy way were one such family. The professor and his weaving wife were certainly another. Susan and Jennifer also. When all this was over, I would have to think about making a life for myself that involved a little more than mocking other people's. This was a new and disturbing responsibility, and I was not sure I welcomed it.

I drained my mug. I needed a break. This last week had been as much as I could cope with for the moment. I would leave my visit to the old lady and tricky questions at *Whilloes* until next week. Tomorrow I would hover on the outskirts of Davina Michener's funeral in case there was something of interest to see, but I would leave the weekend free for sex with Susan. At least it would be different. Sex and home baking. However, now I was in London, and London was where I could find Melissa.

It was six months now. Time to enquire, at the very least. Surely by now she would want to talk. As for sex - well, perhaps she was ready again for the real thing. No offence, of course. Sex between two women must have a lot to offer for those who felt that way. But nevertheless. Back at the flat in Bayswater I rang a disappointed Susan to tell her of my intention to remain in town for the night. Would I be back for the weekend? Yes, I said.

"Promise?"

"Yes, I promise."

I put down the phone. So, I had promised. I called Melissa now, but there was no answer. I tried the studio. Some PA confirmed she would be reading the late bulletin. Could she come to the phone? No, she was busy working on news stories and could not be interrupted. I dropped the phone back on its rest and swore. Colourful, obscene and satisfying.

There was a bottle of bourbon on the sideboard. It looked inviting. I rummaged in the cupboard for a small tot-sized tumbler of the kind always used in Westerns by unshaven and brooding hobos before the big fight in which they wreck the saloon. Filling it, I tossed the honey gold spirit of Kentucky down my throat in one go. It was remarkably satisfying, so I poured again. Once more, the fireball plunged to my guts. Exercising self-control, I screwed the cap back on the bottle (didn't the bottles have corks in the Westerns?) and made my way to the shower. After a clean-up, I would go out to dinner and try Melissa again later in the evening.

Showered and clad in a clean shirt, I thought it might be just worthwhile to try Melissa once more before going out. She was still busy on her news stories. I was beginning to regret the decision to stay up. I meandered along the road to the Italian place I always used and ate spaghetti bolognaise without much enthusiasm. I drank a little wine, but not much, unable to shake off the unsettled feeling which was slowly lapping over me like a rising tide. About twenty minutes before the news was due I rang Melissa again from the payphone outside the restaurant lavatory. Still not available. I am not sure what happened after that. I was increasingly fed up, so I took myself off to the nearest pub.

Later, I went to Melissa's flat in Kensington. It was in darkness, so I hovered in the shadows, carrying out just the sort of peeping project for myself which I had always refused to do for *Whilloes*. At about twenty past eleven a car drew up. Melissa climbed out followed by the make-up girl. They were laughing together. As they went inside the building Melissa took the girl's arm. I turned, spat into the gutter and hailed a passing cab. I had had enough.

CHAPTER EIGHT

The following morning I woke up late with a headache. I tried the traditional remedy of an egg beaten up with worcester sauce, gagged on the first sip and threw the rest down the sink. I had to suffer the usual jams getting out of London, which delayed my arrival in Beechurst until after the funeral had begun. I waited under the trees in a corner of the churchyard and watched the proceedings from a distance.

In due course the mourners trooped out into the autumn gloom, mostly in black but with some grey. Martin was there looking suave and composed. Nearby, Elderflower leaned on a stick supported by his daughter Rosa. Beside her was a stocky, muscular man whom I took to be her Hungarian husband. The procession made its way to the open grave, which surprisingly was in the Mynot sector. They had clearly decided that the union with the Micheners had not proved a success.

I began to identify the Mynots. There was a tall, white haired man with a craggy face, in his early seventies, with a small, sobbing woman too heavily veiled to see her features, on his arm. I took it that these were Davina's parents. Behind, stood a lone figure, shorter than the white haired man, with broad, slightly familiar features. His hair was grey, but by no means white. Instinct told me this was Titus. Other Mynots of various ages and infirmities gathered around, with a good smattering of farm workers and other people from the village. I noticed Susan at the back of the throng. Neville Balcombe, the vicar, was in the process of his dust-to-dust routine, when I became aware that someone was standing next to me. It was Chief Inspector Bridgenorth.

"Melancholy affairs, funerals," he remarked.

"They are meant to be," I responded coolly.

"No, they are meant to be solemn. They turn out melancholy."

I was surprised by this rather profound observation from the inspector. I was making the fatal error of assuming this policeman to be thick.

He turned to me. "How are your enquiries going, Mr Whilloe?"

I looked at him. "Enquiries?"

"You seem to be asking a lot of questions around and about."

"Oh, I see. Well...," I struggled for an answer, "it's a private matter, really. I'm supposed to be writing a book, but I just became interested in this tragic affair."

"Murder is never private."

"No, I suppose not."

"How well do you know an engraver called William Kapowski?"

I was taken completely by surprise. "Kapowski?" I was struggling again and Bridgenorth knew it. "Well, I don't really. I've just met him a couple of times. He was recommended to me to engrave a ring."

Bridgenorth stared at me and said nothing.

I could not hide my curiosity. "Why do you ask, anyway?"

The Inspector watched me closely as he spoke, "He was found dead yesterday afternoon, shortly after a person answering your description, Mr Whilloe, left his workshop."

I almost choked. "Dead? How?"

"A blow to the head, it seems. My colleagues at Scotland Yard have no doubt that it was murder."

"Jesus!"

Bridgenorth's eye was unblinking. I swallowed. My heart was pounding, fit to burst.

"Inspector, you are surely not suggesting..." I could not finish the sentence.

"No one is suggesting anything, Mr Whilloe. Policemen, especially these days, concentrate on the evidence."

My brain, blown apart by the shock of this news, was beginning to reassemble its pieces and focus again. It would be dangerous to play games with this policeman whom I had badly underestimated.

"Inspector, could we talk?"

"I think that would be an excellent idea, Mr Whilloe. If you would care to come to Headquarters straightaway, you could help us with our enquiries. I have a car waiting."

"Am I under arrest?"

"Not at present."

As I followed him across the churchyard and down the path to the waiting car, a trickle of sweat ran down my back.

I was kept at the murder headquarters in Chichester for over six hours. In the car I had made up my mind to tell Chief Inspector Bridgenorth everything, except the visit to Professor Tewkesbury and his theory of aggressive spiritual exchange. In this critical situation I could not run the risk of having my sanity doubted. The inspector took careful notes of my story, but I was not asked to make a statement. He was a much better trained interrogator than I expected, showing interest and sympathy without betraying any sense of the value which he might place on anything I said. He gave no hint of how much he believed. Neither did he give away how much he knew, but I had the uncomfortable feeling that he knew rather more than I did.

There were some tricky moments. He let me know that the valuables stolen from The Grange were found in Kapowski's safe. Paddy Flynn had correctly identified Kapowski as the man who handled that type of merchandise, but I realised that there was mounting evidence to suggest that I had taken the stuff there myself. I tried to press my theory that Martin was the killer. The inspector looked up from his notes.

"I am always interested in other people's theories, Mr Whilloe, but why do you suppose that a man in Mr Michener's financial position, according to our enquiries worth something in the order of a hundred million, should steal his wife's jewellery worth a few thousand pounds and murder her in the process?"

"That's what we have to find out," I said lamely.

I was not arrested, nor was I cautioned. Apart from the absence of motive, the case against me looked almost watertight for the murder of Kapowski. Even with Davina I could see that I was a more plausible killer than Martin, but in the end the inspector closed his notebook and brought the meeting to a conclusion.

"You have been frank and helpful, Mr Whilloe. I need not detain you longer, but we will keep in touch."

It was shortly after five when Bridgenorth himself drove me back to Beechurst, to the church car park where I had left the Morgan. For the journey he kept the conversation away from the crime. It turned out that he, too, had read my book. He seemed quite impressed with my investigative analysis.

As we drew into the car park he made a point of thanking me for my cooperation, then he said, "Murder enquiries are for the police. I know you may sense that you can scoop a story here, but you would be wise to leave the investigation to us, otherwise you may get into deeper water than you are already. I hardly need to tell you that your position is, how shall we say, delicate."

I nodded and thanked him. As I got out of the car and walked across to the Morgan he wound down his window and called after me, "Mr Whilloe," I turned, "be careful."

The inspector swung the wheel and accelerated into the road. I was now certain he knew more than he was giving away. I felt less threatened by the prospect of arrest, but more disturbed by the fear of something else which I could not at that point define.

When I reached Briar Cottage Jennifer had already set off for her weekend away. Susan greeted me with tea and cake in the kitchen. She was wearing an over-large chunky sweater and jeans, having changed out of her funeral clothes. There was nothing funereal about her manner. It turned out that she had taken a chance and booked a table for two at a cottage restaurant in one of the nearby villages, which had a French chef and a high reputation. I suspected the prices might be high as well. Susan had said I was going as her guest, but I reckoned I would have an opportunity to change that. I was pleased at the idea anyway. I needed a diversion to take my mind off the six uncomfortable hours in police headquarters.

It was time for a bath and a change. Having checked the hot water situation with my landlady, I took my blazer and flannels out of the wardrobe. It would do to pay the compliment of smartening up if I were being taken out for a treat.

The soak in the bath helped relax my taut nerves. Back in the bedroom I stood in my bathrobe, thinking of Susan. Behind me the door opened softly, and I sensed rather than felt her draw close to me. Her hands slid beneath my robe.

"I thought you would be ready," she whispered in my ear.

As I turned towards her, she slipped the garment over my shoulders so that it dropped to the floor. She was already naked. Entwined we fell to the bed. Our passion, through long abstinence, was urgent.

"Wow!" I said eventually.
Susan giggled. "Wow to you, too."

CHAPTER NINE

The restaurant was full of low beams and flickering candles which created an intimacy which suited us that night. It was patronised by the well-to-do, or better said, the doing well. There were perhaps too many new clothes with show-off additions which glittered too expensively in the candlelight for my taste, but I was too wrapped in Susan to care.

In the few days I had known Susan, she had turned from a predictable expert in apple pie and tasty gravies, into a vivacious and daring lover, for whom lust was again stirring in my loins before we were halfway through the meal. We began to talk, and as, I suppose, is natural for newly consummated lovers, we talked about ourselves. Susan asked me about my childhood and upbringing, and I told her of the privilege and remoteness of my early years. She asked me whether my parents were still alive, and when I nodded she leant forward.

"Tell me, St John, what are your mother and father like?"

She put great emphasis on the last word. I understood that she was asking about them as people, not what they looked like. I was flustered to discover I hardly knew the answer. Somehow, I had never given them much thought.

"Well," I began, "my father is a retired solicitor in his early seventies. He occasionally pops into the firm but it's really run by my eldest brother. He is kind, but very correct. He sees everything within the constraints of the rules of his class."

"And your mother?"

"Much the same. Neither of them has ever had to think about money, or if so, only to reign in extravagance. She spends her days at bridge and committees, not unlike the gentry around here."

"Yes, but what was she like as a mother?"

"A mother? She was all right. She always made sure I knew what to do and how to behave. I was fed and clothed. I have no complaints. I have never been really close to my parents. Maybe that is because I was adopted."

"Is that why you are a rebel?"

"Maybe."

"No matter," she replied munching, "I like rebels."

I returned the compliment of asking about her parents. They had clearly been a close family with a lot of interaction and love and mutual support. Her father had been something grey in an insurance company, but the up-side of this was that he persuaded her husband to insure his life generously, which was the source of Susan's financial independence. When she returned to her childhood village after Craig's death, she took on the pearls and tweed image to blend into the community because she knew that was how people were. Hanging in the closet of her psyche was a sharper, more assertive profile and I was beginning to catch sight of this now.

When we returned to Briar Cottage we made love again. This time it was less frantic. We undressed each other slowly, item by item. I was able to take a proper look at Susan's body. Her breasts were quite small, but she had much bigger hips and thighs than Melissa. Her ankles and feet were small and neat, as were her hands. She was not fat, but her bones were certainly well-covered. Melissa's figure was very much that of the high class pin-up. Largish breasts, small hips, long, slender thighs. Susan's skin was white. Melissa was permanently tanned from frequent holidays in sunny places and a sunbed in between.

There was something natural and spontaneous about Susan's approach to sex which I found refreshing and warm. There was no doubt that Melissa was a good lover, but it was a technique which she had acquired through careful study and practice. She was able to project the senses to undreamed of levels of experience, but left the emotions flat. With Susan, making love was a fun experience which was physical rather than just erotic. In the end, I felt with Melissa I was having sex the correct way as sex therapists would recommend. Like the neutral accent which she had paid to acquire, everything about Melissa was what she thought it ought to be, rather than what she was. Melissa was merchandised, but Susan was genuine.

We spent a lot of that weekend is the bedroom, but we did other things, too. We walked on the downs, shrouded in mist and low cloud, listening to the echoes of passing life drifting up from an invisible world below. We drove to the sea where we stood arm in arm alone upon the shingle, watching the never-ending arrival of the curling waves which threw themselves with a thud upon the beach, disintegrating into a torrent of white foam. Grey water stretched white-capped as far as the eye could see, to merge into an opaque horizon which melted into the sky. Above us the melancholy cries of circling gulls echoed, as shack-like dwellings, strung out along the unmade road which bordered the beach, waited forlorn for the return of the sun, of warmth, of inhabitants, of the pulse of life itself. We stood there, absorbing the sights and sounds, wrapped against the chill and dusted by the salt spray of the sea.

On the Saturday evening we went to the theatre in Chichester and saw a promising new play whose promoters hoped would move on to the West End. It turned out to be something of a meander through the emotions and sensibilities of a rather annoying couple, who stayed the course of our glimpse into their life together, mostly because they were too scared to break apart. I rather enjoyed it, but I think Susan would have preferred a more sharply defined plot. She told me over a curry afterwards that she had hoped the one was going to murder the other, and we had a good laugh.

As the short weekend sped by, although we were both warm for each other's company, we kept telling each other not to expect too much. This was for now. Neither of us could see the future. I left for London late on Sunday afternoon. I wanted to catch Gerard at the office early the following morning, and I preferred to avoid the commuter traffic. There was another reason at the back of my mind. Jennifer would be returning later in the evening and I thought it best if Susan were able to concentrate on her daughter.

When I reached Lincoln's Inn the next morning I was put out to discover that Gerard was not expected until ten thirty. Having made sure his secretary would call me as soon as he arrived, I told her to tell him it was urgent family business, which would frighten him into thinking I had done something awful and make sure he saw me straightaway. I took the lift to my attic. Janice was pleased to see me. We had been out of touch for over a week, but that was not unusual.

The flow of post to my office was never to the level of a cascade, but there had been one or two items of interest which Janice laid out for me to read. There was a letter from a small firm of specialist publishers who produce user-friendly books of how to do this and that, who wondered if I might be interested in writing a small volume about unit trust investment. It sounded excruciatingly dull, so I told Janice to write and say that I was too busy on other assignments to give it the attention which it deserved, but please feel free to ask again. There was another from the financial editor of one of the quality Sundays who wanted me to investigate a certain investment manager and financial adviser who was believed to be pocketing generous slices of his clients' fortunes. As many of these were both well-known and well off, but also reticent about their money and keen not to attract publicity over the matter, there was a powerful chance he would get away with it. This sounded much more fun. I composed a letter for Janice to send, provisionally accepting but requiring a delay of ten days before I could start so as to complete the assignment on which I was presently engaged.

When Janice asked me what this was exactly, I had no difficulty in being rather vague because I could find no way of describing it properly, even to myself. I remembered to ask her whether Mrs Michener (I did not bother to explain that she was not Mrs Michener at all) had rung or written for her appointment. It turned out she had rung. Not that this proved anything.

By now Gerard had arrived and his secretary phoned to say he would see me now, but I would have to be quick as he had important meetings to attend. I have no patience with people who turn up late and then declare themselves to be in a hurry, so I ignored the lift and made my way down the several flights of stairs to the partners' floor at a leisurely pace. I found my elder brother sipping coffee and smoking a cigarette. He greeted me with some impatience. I came straight to the point.

"You told me the other day that we didn't act for the Micheners, but apparently we act for Dorothy Skillette, who is, in fact, Dorothy Michener."

Gerard, who had started reading his post, looked up sharply.

"I'm sorry, I did not make the connection. We always talk of her here as Skillette, rather than Michener."

"How long have we acted for her?"

"Years and years. She was father's secretary originally."

This was news.

"Really? I had been told she was old man Michener's secretary."

"That came afterwards, apparently."

"How did she become our client?"

"I have no idea, St John. It was before I came into the firm, but mostly father advised her about her financial affairs. She had been rather cut off by her own family and had scant resources."

"I gather we now pay her fees at some fancy old people's home."

"Yes, we do."

"How do we do that out of scant resources?"

"Ah," said Gerard, "she inherited some money."

"Did some dying Skillette relent?"

"No, I don't think so. This happened before father finally retired when he was still coming in a few days a week to look after certain of the old clients. Dorothy Skillette was one of them."

"Do you know who left her the money?"

"I have no idea. You would have to ask father. St John, why are you asking all these questions about this woman?"

"I'm not quite sure at the moment, but she seems to be connected with the story I'm investigating." Gerard had been pretty tight with his own information, so I saw no reason to be forthcoming at this stage.

Gerard grunted. "Poking around in people's pasts is very rarely a good idea, St John."

Gerard went back to his post, puffing on his cigarette. I felt this was as far as I was going to get. Indeed, I was not sure he knew any more. He sipped his coffee, but there was no suggestion of offering me a cup.

"Well, I'll be off," I said, "thanks for your help."

On the way to the lift, it was all right to walk down but up was another matter, I passed the office of Gerard's secretary, an obnoxious, snooty girl called Priscilla. I poked my head around the door. "Thanks for the coffee," I said airily.

Startled, she looked up from her word processor. Words were forming on her lips, but I was along the passage and out of earshot before they became a sound.

Upstairs, I signed the letters to the publishing house and the editor, blew Janice a kiss and left the building. It had been my intention to drive up to Lincoln, but I changed my plans. First, I wanted to have another talk with Rosa.

Two hours later I sat at the kitchen table at The Grange. The big white cup with steaming black coffee was before me, and this time a piece of Rosa's home-made fruitcake. I did not have to waste time beating around the bush. Rosa knew by now I was fishing for information, and I think she had already decided to talk.

"How well did Davina and Martin get on?"

Rosa shrugged her ample shoulders. Her high cheekbones caused little mounds of flesh to protrude beneath her eyes, and these were now slightly flushed.

"Not that well. I think it was worse after his father, Arnold, died and they moved in here. Davina liked the village because she had been brought up nearby, but she hated this house. She said it made her irritable and depressed."

"What about Martin?"

"Oh, he loves it. He treats it, well, he treats it almost as a shrine. After his father died he carefully restored it to the way it was in his grandfather's day."

That was odd for a young man. He should be looking to the future, not the past.

"Did he remember what it was like?"

"A little, but my old father did, and so did I. So we gave him a lot of advice. It wasn't very difficult."

"So he's relaxed when he is here?"

"Oh yes, most certainly, although he's not here that often, because the business keeps him away."

This was very strange. The fake Davina seemed to have given me a mirror image of what was going on at The Grange.

"Do you know if they wanted children?"

"Oh dear yes, that was a problem." Rosa spread her hands. "They were both tested, and nobody could find anything wrong, but nothing seemed to happen. Martin became really agitated because of the will."

"The will?"

I could see Rosa was wondering whether she was telling me too much, but she poured us more coffee and went on to tell me that after old Stanley's death, Arnold had felt that the family had treated Dorothy Skillette very badly. He often said so when family matters were being discussed. He felt some sort of provision should have been made for the baby.

"Does anyone know what happened to the baby?" I interrupted.

"Well, no. That's the point I'll come to in a minute."

Rosa hesitated, then continued to explain that the problem weighed more heavily on Arnold's mind as he grew older, and eventually he decided to add a codicil to his will. Arnold had inherited from Stanley and originally planned to leave everything to Martin, with various technical provisions to reduce inheritance taxes. Anyway, towards the end, he decided he wanted to leave twenty-five per cent of the Company to Dorothy Skillette's child with the additional proviso that if Martin should die without issue, the whole thing would go to this unknown person. He discussed it with Martin who was furious, and there were endless rows.

"Arnold was a very stubborn man, and I believe only dug his heels in because he didn't want his mind changed by his son," Rosa explained.

For a housekeeper Rosa knew an awful lot, but it was clear that the Michener set-up was really one big family, and I suspected that what she had not been told she had picked up from hearing the rows.

"Was the codicil added?" I asked urgently, unable to contain my excitement.

"Yes, but there was a compromise. It was agreed that Dorothy Skillette's offspring would only acquire these rights of inheritance if he or she claimed them before the end of the year in which this person became thirty-five. As the baby was more or less the same age as Martin, the deadline expires at the end of this year."

This was a strange condition with a hint of melodrama. The stuff of Victorian novelette. I said as much to Rosa.

"We all thought it complicated at the time. It was Martin's idea. I think he saw it as a way of satisfying his father's guilt on behalf of his grandfather, knowing there was little to no chance of the claim ever being made."

I thought for a bit.

"If the child was Titus Mynot's, doesn't *he* know where the person is now?"

Rosa shook her head. "You must remember that Titus has always denied his involvement with Dorothy."

"What about the adoption agency?"

"Ah," said Rosa, "that was all very secret. Nobody knows what happened to the child. It was arranged through the clinic in Harley Street where Dorothy gave birth."

"Why all the secrecy?" I asked.

Rosa hesitated. "Scandal, I suppose."

"Was it a boy or a girl?"

Again the hesitation. "No one knows."

Maybe. Maybe not. I felt Rosa knew more than she admitted. A thought suddenly flashed through my mind that perhaps the girl who had pretended to be Davina was the child, but I had judged her to be much younger. I had, of course, met her only once and could have been mistaken. Classy women are adept at disguising their age, and she could have been adopted by some wealthy family, which would fit in with the discreet little clinic in Harley Street. Bastards for the well-to-do. Such an outfit could have conducted a nifty little trade, passing the peccadilloes of one upper crust family into legitimisation with another. The by-product of passion before the pill.

This visit to Rosa's kitchen had given me good reasons for a lurking threat to the progeny of Dorothy's elicit affair, but there was still something more I wanted to ask. I decided to be direct. I drained my cup and set it carefully in its saucer, then without looking at Rosa, spoke slowly.

"Rosa, do you think Martin killed his wife?"

I looked up. She, who had been looking at me, looked down.

"Well," she said, fingering her wedding ring in a nervous preoccupied gesture, "I think he was here that morning. Joseph saw someone."

"Joseph?"

"My husband."

"Ah. Has he told the police?"

"No."

"Will he?"

"No."

Rosa looked up at me.

"All of us in this family, and we regard ourselves as one family, have been through terrible things in our earlier lives. We owe so much to each other. We will stick together no matter what. None of us would be here but for old Stanley. We could never betray his grandson."

I got up from the table, walked around to where Rosa was sitting, lifted her hand and kissed it gently.

"I understand," I said softly.

I had a feeling Rosa had carefully prepared, almost rehearsed all she had told me that morning. There was a fluency relating to complicated family matters, even legal terms, which seemed out of character for someone who was, after all, the housekeeper. Then again, she had lived a relatively sophisticated life in the Michener household where staff and family merged.

She looked at me and smiled. There were tears in her eyes.

As I made my way down the front path to the tradesman's gate, I looked at the date on my watch. It was November 1. The thirty-fifth year had not long to run. If I were to find Dorothy Skillette's child and help that person to lay claim to a fortune, I would have to hurry. I was now sure that Martin would hurry to stop the claim by any means, including murder.

I found Briar Cottage empty, but this suited me. I wanted time to think and make notes. I was beginning to see threads that lead somewhere. Dorothy Skillette was coming somewhat more to life. It was a strange coincidence that she had been my father's secretary, but that explained today's connection with *Whilloes*. New interest now surrounded the identity of the fake Davina. In many ways it would fit if she turned out to be Dorothy Skillette's daughter. I was pretty sure that Martin had murdered the real Davina and I had no doubt whatever he had killed Willy Kapowski. Yet if Willy was as reliable as he said he was, there was no need to do this, and why leave the incriminating jewels in the safe? I had the disturbing feeling that Martin was trying to frame me for the crime, yet I could not see why. I would need to be on my guard. He was not far behind me.

That evening at dinner with Jennifer present I behaved as the respectable lodger, and Susan acted the part of the decorous landlady, except when she squeezed my bottom when we were alone for a moment in the kitchen. I was grateful for the weekend. It had done me no end of good, but now I needed to steer clear of Susan emotionally until I had resolved the mystery surrounding the Micheners.

CHAPTER TEN

I left early the following morning. I planned to stop at Somerset House en route for Lincoln. I thought a sight of Arnold Michener's strange will would bear fruit. I am not going to describe the hanging about and to-ing and fro-ing that takes place at Somerset House if you want to have a sight of old documents. Sufficient to say it is best not to be in a hurry.

It was nearly midday by the time I had copies of both Arnold and Stanley Michener's wills. It was Arnold's I was interested in, but I thought Stanley's might have some bearing on it. Clutching these I made my way to the Iron Duke and sat down with Paddy, who was in his usual seat. After giving him the news, which he knew already, of Willy Kapowski's murder, and an envelope with cash for his additional services which I would shortly employ, I sent him off to get the drinks and a couple of ploughman's. Over beer and stilton I read through pages of legalese, with endless paragraphs without punctuation, but I found what I wanted to know and a bit extra as well.

The Michener custom was for the living, while still in good health, to pass the bulk of their assets to the next in line, so as to outlive the qualification period and significantly reduce the impact of death duties. In addition, about sixty per cent of the shares of Michener Group had been placed in trust by old Stanley for Arnold and his issue, which in the event, turned out to be Martin alone. In spite of all these arrangements, it appeared that Arnold still personally owned about twenty-five per cent of Michener Group shares when he died. It was these which he left by codicil to the unnamed and unidentified child of Dorothy Michener, née Skillette. The codicil contained the onerous condition that the child had to identify itself and make the claim.

Then came two surprises. By another codicil dated the day before his own death, Arnold had removed this requirement and imposed a rather different condition. If the claimant had not come forward by the end of the thirty-fifth year of his or her life, the executors, who were to hold the shares in trust meanwhile, were to take active steps to find the person and release the inheritance. At today's prices this would be worth about twenty-five million. So now it appeared that Arnold, on his death bed, still suffering his father's remorse, decided to ignore his son's demands and change his will. He probably never mentioned it to Martin. Rosa had picked up most of what she knew by listening to the arguments, although I suspected old Elderflower had sharper hearing than he let on. But I was pretty sure that none of them knew of this last minute change. Martin himself would have learned after his father's death. It would put a whole new urgency on his identifying Dorothy's child before the end of this year. After that, it would become an official enquiry by the trustees. Before long , the hated progeny of Titus Mynot would own a quarter of Stanley's company.

There was one other codicil, also dated for the eve of Arnold's death. It was a bequest to Dorothy Michener, née Skillette, of £150,000. This was hardly lavish in the context of Arnold's total assets which were probably in the order of forty million, but it was a gesture certainly, and a timely one at that, because it was shortly afterward that Dorothy had suffered her stroke. The thought then occurred to me that if Stanley had lived to complete the divorce, Dorothy would have received a financial settlement, even as the guilty party. An insignificant sum to the hugely wealthy Stanley would have been substantial to her in her straightened circumstances, cut off as she was from her own family. I had no doubt at all that if my father had been advising her, *Whilloes* would certainly have been able to win her financial security. So it looked as if she had deliberately not sought any financial support. This was curious. It made the old lady's inability to communicate all the more frustrating.

Paddy remained dutifully silent while my eyes and mind worked through all this material. When I finished I went to the bar for refills. As Paddy quaffed his beer and sipped the accompanying Jack Daniels, I asked if anything was known about the Kapowski murderer. It was definitely an outsider, he assured me. None of the professionals would have harmed him because he was too useful to them. This led me to an assignment for Paddy. It had crossed my mind that Martin must have had a connection with Willy Kapowski that had nothing to do with burglaries. The fact that Willy had a Polish background was potentially significant.

"Paddy, did you tell me that Kapowski's parents were killed in the blitz?"

"That's right."

"He was not old enough to be on his own. Who brought him up?"

"I think he was fostered."

"Do you know by whom?"

"No, but I could find out."

"Paddy, I need to know all you can find out about those foster parents. If they are still alive, go and see them and check out any connection with the Michener family."

By the time I had finished with Paddy it was nearly three, and past six before I reached the outskirts of Lincoln. I came to the conclusion that it was too late in the day to visit Dorothy. She would not be much good in any event, but she would be at her best early in the morning. I pulled into a service station and bought a toothbrush and some toothpaste. It was a blessing on these occasions not to have to worry about shaving.

I looked around for a place to stay. I decided against a new antiseptic sprawl on the fringe of the A1, which offered everything for the passing traveller including conference facilities and a health club. I made my way into the town centre where I was soon settled in a comfortable little two star inn off Westgate which had a secure car park at the rear so that the Morgan would be comfortable, too. I checked the dining room menu. It was a bit chippy, grills mostly, so I ventured out to see if I could do better.

I happened upon an excellent little Chinese where I was waited on attentively and enjoyed an excellent meal. Disappointingly the place was quite empty, save for a girl in her late twenties, crisply suited for business, with an open briefcase, a filofax and a mobile phone which rang during the meal, into which she spoke earnestly but too far away for me to overhear. I found her rather attractive in a bossy sort of way. Twice during the evening she smiled at me, and I believed we both came to the conclusion we could pick each other up. But I had enough women in my life at the moment, which was in turmoil anyway. So when her phone rang again, I took the opportunity to beat a hasty retreat, after paying my bill in cash by tossing notes onto the table American style and leaving without waiting for the change.

Back at the two star, I propped up the bar for a further hour and drank a few beers before climbing into bed, which was high, old-fashioned and soft. This was probably not ideal for patrons with back problems, but I slept soundly until the clatter of the new day's activity woke me at seven the next morning.

After breakfast I drove southeast towards the Lincolnshire fens. The Bulmer Retreat, as it was called, was about fifteen miles out in flat country, surrounded by a well-organised plantation of oak and beech. The property could be described as a mansion, originally with about ten bedrooms, but fell well short of a stately home. Dating from the very early Victorian period, it was everything that The Grange was not. Soft geometric lines framed its simple facade in perfect proportion. The architect was confident and restrained, quite unlike the bombastic show-off who had created the Michener property at the end of the old Queen's reign.

I had phoned the evening before, so when the front door was opened to my knock, I was expected. I was taken to the matron first, a robust woman in her late forties, who evidently combined medical and nursing skills with a head for business. She extended a hand.

"Mr Whilloe, it's so nice to see you. Mrs Michener will be pleased. She doesn't receive many visitors. I believe you are from her solicitors?"

I nodded. "Indirectly, yes. I was passing, so it seemed a good idea to call."

"Of course. Let me take your coat."

She held out her hand for the stockman, and after hanging it on a stand in her office, presumably to ensure that I had to call in before leaving, she led me along a passage.

"Dorothy is still in her room. Later in the morning, we take her through to the sunroom with the others."

"How many other residents do you have?" I asked.

"Just ten."

I grunted. The establishment was clearly very exclusive.

"They all have their own rooms," continued the matron, "Dorothy's is on the ground floor because it makes it easier for her wheelchair. We have an electric platform lift, but it's really for the walkers who need a little help to get upstairs."

She turned, offering me a flamboyant smile, as she opened the door to a large room with big sash windows which reached almost to the floor. There was a bed and two easy chairs as well as the usual paraphernalia associated with an invalid.

Dorothy Skillette sat in her wheelchair looking out of the window which faced to the side of the room, so my first sight of her was in profile. A shaft of sunlight caught her face as we walked in, illuminating a high, noble brow and a straight, sharp nose. The features were etched in determined lines, and at once I recognised a kindred, though now dormant, spirit. This was the face of a rebel. The matron, Mrs Bulmer I later discovered was her name, she apparently owned everything, strode purposefully across the room and talked to the old lady as if she could understand. Maybe she could. It was encouraging to see Dorothy was not treated as a vegetable.

"Dorothy dear, you have a visitor this morning. A gentleman has come to see you. A Mr Whilloe."

The old lady turned her head quite sharply towards me. So, she did understand. Mrs Bulmer pulled forward a chair.

"I expect you would like some coffee, Mr Whilloe? I'll have some sent in."

I whispered to her, "How much does she understand?"

"We can't be sure, but it's best if you just talk to her normally."

I sat down close to her. I began by saying what a lovely room she had, and how nice to look out over the gardens, which were indeed worth looking at. They were beautifully maintained and looked as if they had been preserved as originally laid out in the last century. A maid brought in coffee and biscuits, but there was only one cup.

"What about Miss Skillette?" I asked.

"She will have hers a little later," explained the maid. "A nurse will give it to her in a feeding cup."

I nodded. I went on to talk about my father and my two brothers, and how the firm was running, all of which I thought might strike a chord with her early years. She watched me closely. The expression of her eyes seeming to hover in a no-man's land midway between comprehension and vacancy. After about half an hour I decided to try to break through. I told her that I had recently visited The Grange. I spoke a little of Stanley Michener and his firm. I leant quite close to her and took her hand in mine. It was warm and soft.

"Dorothy, can you remember your child?"

There was a subtle change to the expression of her eyes. I felt they had moved nearer comprehension. I put another question.

"Do you know what happened to the child?"

For a moment there was nothing, then her hand squeezed mine. I was astonished. She did know. I asked the question again. She squeezed once more. The corner of her mouth quivered, but this was as far as I was able to get. There were no further signs of recognition or understanding, and I felt it best to move from the subject. After a few more minutes I made my excuses, promising before I could stop myself to call again. Her eyes followed me to the door, which I closed with care.

I found the effusive Mrs Bulmer attending to papers in her office. She helped me on with my coat.

"How did you find her?"

"Better than I expected."

"Yes, we feel now that she is making a little progress. The doctors are quite hopeful."

"Tell me, Mrs Bulmer, you mentioned she doesn't have many visitors. Who else comes to see her?"

Her shrewd eyes looked at me from behind her reading glasses, weighing the desire to show off knowledge with the need for discretion. She spoke softly, but in the earnest tones of a gossip.

"Well, it's interesting that you ask. In fact, the only person who ever comes to see her is her niece, Clare Skillette. She comes once every two or three months. Poor Dorothy seems to have been disowned by her own family and that of her late husband. Your firm, of course, pays the fees."

At least I had a small piece of information. This Clare Skillette would not be too difficult to find. Mrs Bulmer escorted me to the front door.

"Oh," she said, as I stepped out in the sunlight, "there was one other caller, about six months ago. Her step grandson, apparently, a Mr Martin Michener. Unfortunately poor Dorothy seemed very upset by his visit, so we asked him not to call again."

"Ah," I said, "I see."

I looked at my watch. If I drove fast I could reach the Iron Duke in time to see Paddy. He would probably have news for me about the Kapowski family, but most important, he could help me locate the old lady's niece, Clare. The more I thought about this girl, the more I convinced myself this was the old lady's child. She had been cut off by the Skillette's. It was very unlikely that an odd niece would keep contact, but her daughter, masquerading as her niece, would. Many adopted children knew exactly who their parents were. In view of the strange circumstances surrounding this affair, it was quite likely that Clare would have maintained contact with her mother. The critical thing now was to get to her before Martin Michener. He had already tried to wring the information from the old lady, so he was well on the trail. There was no time to lose.

I became so hyped up with my theory as I drove down the A1, that I pulled in to a service area and phoned the Iron Duke to leave a message for Paddy to wait for me. Sure enough, I found him sitting expectantly in the usual place. He had already bought me a bourbon, with the ice in a separate glass. His watery eyes twinkled.

"I wasn't sure how long you'd be. I didn't want it to melt in the drink. Watered drinks are bad for the soul!"

This time we did not bother with food. Around us, trendy people smoked, drank and shouted at each other to make themselves heard.

"You were right, Jack."

"About what?"

"Stanley Michener helped Kapowski. The boy was fostered. When he left school Stanley financed his apprenticeship. It seems the old man kept an eye on his fellow countrymen in need."

"Did you find out about the foster parents?"

"Yes. The father was a bus driver, died a few years back. Mother is still alive, lives in a supervised flat for the elderly in Hackney."

"Did she work?"

"Yes."

"What as?"

"A nurse. But it's not what she did; it's where she did it."

"How do you mean?"

"She worked at the clinic in Harley Street, where Dorothy Skillette had the baby."

This was a stroke of luck.

"Have you talked to her?"

"Yup!" Paddy looked at his empty glass.

I pushed through the crush for refills. When I got back he told me the rest. Like everything else so far, it was tantalising enough to be interesting but fell short of what I wanted. Kapowski's foster mother remembered Dorothy as a patient, but she did not nurse her. The baby was whisked away at birth, so she did not know where it went to or whether it was a boy or girl. She did remember one thing, however. The arrangements had been fixed up with a solicitor. Word went around the clinic that this was an especially hush-hush case. The staff speculated that the father was somebody famous.

"Did she remember which solicitor?"

"No, she wasn't sure she had ever heard the name. I mentioned your firm, but it didn't mean anything to her."

I had just started to tell Paddy about Dorothy's niece when the barman shouted to him that he was wanted on the telephone. He went off to take it, but was back quickly.

"It was Janice from your office trying to find you."

"Find me?"

"Yes. She's had a phone call and wants to talk to you about it."

"Did she say who from?"

"Clare Skillette."

CHAPTER ELEVEN

Dragging Paddy by the arm, I was out of the Iron Duke like a bat out of hell, pushing through the boozing throng as I forced a passage to the door. I had been lucky enough to find a meter for the Morgan earlier, and we ran to it. Paddy was tall and had difficulty getting his legs in, but we sped off into the traffic in the little car and made for Lincoln's Inn Fields at full speed.

There, we emptied our pockets of pound coins to guarantee two penalty free hours, and the two of us were quickly standing breathless and sweaty in front of a surprised Janice. We had run all the way up the stairs because the lift was being serviced. Paddy was in quite a state. His arteries and liver were very sub-standard after all the drinking. He sank down on the chesterfield, moving his position quickly as a spring found its mark. Janice handed him a coffee. She gave me a cup as well, but I was too excited to drink it.

"When did this girl ring, Janice? What did she say? Where is she?"

Janice, who was clearly enjoying the excitement, made me sit on the chesterfield next to Paddy, which I did but very gingerly.

"There's not a lot to tell. She said her name was Clare Skillette, that you would know who she was, and that she wanted to meet you because she had some information you would find helpful."

"Did you make an appointment?"

"Yes. Tomorrow at three at the Sloane Tower Hotel."

This was surprising. The Sloane Tower is one of those ultra expensive international hotels which the native English avoid, largely because they cannot afford it.

"Whereabouts?"

"At her office. I presume she works there."

That was easy to check. I rang the hotel and asked for Clare Skillette. Immediately I was put through to the marketing department. No, she was not available. She was in Paris and would not be back until the following afternoon. I remembered to ask for her title. She was the Assistant Marketing Manager.

I took Paddy through to my office. He wanted to know what was going on. I had only, so far, given him assignments. I had not taken him into my confidence. Now I gave him much the same story as I had given the Chief Inspector. He agreed that it was really frustrating that I would have to wait till the following day to meet the star witness who might hold the key to the mystery. But there really was no option. This Clare was obviously a quite high-powered career executive type. I became more than ever convinced that she was the daughter of Dorothy and Titus Mynot. She would learn that she was worth tens of millions, but if she were to enjoy her fortune, we must hope that Chief Inspector Bridgenorth and his colleagues would find the evidence which would put Martin Michener safely behind bars. To be sure that happened, I needed to come up with something which would prove that I was not the culprit they were after.

I looked at Paddy. "How long would it take us to drive up to Hackney and see this foster mother? I would like to talk to her a little more."

Paddy shrugged. "About twenty minutes, depending on traffic."

"Let's go," I said.

"Not in your car."

I turned to him. "Why not?"

"In that sort of area you could easily get the hood slashed. We'll take mine."

I was astonished. I didn't think that Paddy drove. Certainly it was not a good idea with his drinking, but he was sober now. It turned out that the crafty so-and-so had a girlfriend who worked for the Inland Revenue in an enormous building around the corner, which had an underground car park for authorised persons only. She had given Paddy her smart card, and when he was the worse for wear she drove him home. To her place, I imagined, but I did not ask.

It was a Ford Fiesta. A bit small for Paddy, but it was ideal for traffic. The Irishman drove like a demon but with great precision. He never missed a space or an opportunity and always arrived at each junction in the right lane. We were at our destination in fifteen minutes, a small block of flats on three floors surrounded by an estate of town houses and tower blocks which soared upwards.

Searing monuments to the destruction of the old residential communities. The sight of it all made me angry.

I was still feeling angry as Doreen Porter opened her front door. We had been let into the building by the warden, but only after Paddy had reminded him of his earlier visit and I had thrust my business card bearing the *Whilloes* address forward.

Mrs Porter should have been grey, but lavish use of henna rinse kept that part of the ageing process at bay. She was quite tall, and although in her late seventies, still had a passable figure. She wore clothes which were obviously inexpensive but chosen with care, and presented an appearance in which she clearly took not a little pride. She had a generous splash of cockney cheerfulness tempered with a practical air which came from her nursing training, as well as a touch of refinement she must have acquired working in establishments like the clinic in Harley Street. She took one look at the florid Paddy and went off to her little kitchen to make tea. She returned with a tray which included a fruit cake. She cut a generous slice for Paddy and made him eat it. He did not argue.

I started by saying how sorry we were about the tragedy of Willy Kapowski. She did not seem too upset by this. Apparently there had been little contact between them over the years, and she knew of his connections with the underworld of which she sternly disapproved.

"I told him many a time that if he mixed with that sort he would come to a sticky end, and that's what has happened."

Eventually I drew the conversation to the clinic and Dorothy Skillette. Paddy had done his job well. She did not appear to be able to remember any more for me than she had told him.

"What makes you so sure that a solicitor was involved?"

"Well, usually the home worked with one or two exclusive adoption agencies, but in this case I know that everything was arranged by a solicitor. He even came with a nurse to collect the baby within a few hours of its birth. This would make tracing the child even more difficult, because there would be no adoption agency records to examine."

I asked her to describe the solicitor, which was difficult for her and meaningless anyway, because we were talking about something that had happened thirty-five years ago. After Paddy had been forced to eat a second piece of cake and we had chatted a little of the ills of the modern world, we left. The Irishman took me back to *Whilloes*.

As I sat behind my desk wondering if Gerard would help me trace the solicitor who had collected the baby, a shrill ring from the telephone snapped the train of my thoughts and brought me back to the present. Janice explained it was Susan on the line. I was surprised. Her voice was tight and anxious.

"Are you coming down tonight?"

"Well, I'm not sure. There are so many things going on up here and I have to be in town again tomorrow. I rather thought it would save a journey to stay at the flat."

"St John, I need to talk to you."

"What about?"

"I cannot say on the phone."

There was fear in her voice. I decided not to press her further.

"I'll leave now. It's the rush hour, so it will take some time."

She sounded relieved.

"Drive carefully. I'll keep supper for you."

Susan and Jennifer had eaten by the time I arrived. Jennifer was doing her homework on the dining room table, so we went into the kitchen. Susan closed the door and took a plate of stew from the oven. I was grateful for the offer of a beer. She took two lagers from the fridge. Opening one she poured two glasses from it.

"Cheers," she said absently.

"What's the problem?"

She looked at me directly. Her eyes were wide and fearful.

"There's a rumour in the village."

"A rumour of what?"

"That you killed Davina."

I stopped the forkful midway to my mouth and put it back on the plate.

"Perhaps that's because I am a stranger. After all, if people do not accept the burglar theory, it has to be someone local. That's not a nice thought. So I would be an easy scapegoat."

"Joseph saw someone."

"Joseph?"

"Rosa's husband."

"Oh! Who did he see?"

"He thinks it was you."

This made no sense. Rosa had told me that Joseph had seen someone but hinted that it was Martin. Was that cursed ménage at The Grange so close that they would frame me to protect the last surviving Michener?

"Well, he can't have seen me because I wasn't here that morning."

"He saw a man. First he thought it was Martin, but now he thinks it was you. He saw your beard."

"My beard?"

This was tricky. My beard was indeed distinctive, and the chance of a burglar having one was remote. But if Martin had gone far enough to disguise himself in my likeness, Davina's killing had been much more pre-planned than I had thought.

"St John, what are you doing here in Beechurst? You do not seem to be writing a book. You were seen leaving the churchyard during Davina's funeral with the police inspector. Hours later he drove you back to your car. Are you some sort of policeman too, or are you under suspicion?"

I looked at Susan. Her face was lined with anxiety. I thought I was close to the solution of this mystery, yet the closer I moved to the answers, deeper was the mess I was getting myself into. I took a swig of the beer and pushed the stew to one side. I took both Susan's hands in mine and squeezed them. She squeezed back tightly.

"I'm going to tell you everything."

I did just that. Aggressive spiritual exchange. Everything. She listened intently and wide-eyed until I had finished. When I stopped she moved around the table and kissed me on the forehead.

"Thank God for that. I knew you were not a killer."

"You believe me then."

"Yes."

"Why?"

"I always thought there was something peculiar about Martin. He and Davina were very alike. They even looked alike in some ways. But Martin has this weird something about him which sets him apart."

"What sort of a something do you see?"

"A sort of magnetism."

"Magnetism? Does that mean he is attractive?"

"In an evil sort of way, yes."

"Put another way, is he sexy?"

"Yes."

"Would you get into his bed if he asked you?"

"Before I met you, I think I would, yes. But not now. I knew that for sure when he called this morning."

"What?!"

"Yes, he called around this morning to thank me for coming to the funeral and for being Davina's friend. Very smarmy, really, but then he told me about Joseph and what he'd seen and warned me to be careful. He suggested it would be wise for me to give you notice to move."

I stood up from the table, almost tipping over the chair.

"Martin here! Jesus, I wish you'd said. He's inventing all that crap about Joseph seeing me. It is Martin whom Joseph saw! The bastard is trying to frame me. And for Kapowski's murder! I'm not sure why, but I think it's because he wants me to lead him to Dorothy Skillette's child. Once I have done that for him he needs to unload both me and his crimes. To parcel us together would be very convenient."

Susan put her arms around my waist. "St John, this is dangerous. It's not just an ordinary crime. Get out while you can."

I shook my head. "I'm nearly there now. I'm going to deliver Dorothy Skillette's child to its fortune and see Martin Michener behind bars. With his wild and mutated psyche, no one will be safe until that is done!"

Susan shrugged. "You really should leave it all to the police, but I know you won't listen to good advice. In the short time I have known you I have learned that!"

I rested my hands on her shoulders. "I am sorry," he said.

"Don't worry," she grinned, "your pigheadedness turns me on!"

That night when I got into bed, I left my pyjamas under the pillow and climbed under the duvet nude. I know what I hoped for, but I hoped in vain. Not in front of Jennifer was a rule of the house. Eventually I fell asleep. When I awoke in the morning it was in a state of anxiety.

CHAPTER TWELVE

I could not face another run up the M23 to London, so Susan took me to the station at Pulborough and I went up by train. It was quite a relaxing experience out of the rush hour. Not too full. Women going shopping mostly, the odd businessman here and there. From Victoria I took the tube to Temple and walked up to Lincoln's Inn. I checked the office to see if there had been any developments. There had not, except a message from Gerard to drop by.

This I did. I caught him just before one of his endless meetings.

"Father has been trying to get in touch with you. He wants to see you."

"I want to see him, too," I responded, "but first I have to see somebody else. Tell him I will call."

"Very well."

I thought Gerard looked rather shifty. For the first time in my life I detected that he was nervous.

I walked down to the Iron Duke for a chinwag with Paddy, but I was careful to have only one drink. I was not hungry because my stomach was churning with the excitement. I asked Paddy to remain there until he heard from me. The pub was open all day.

"At all costs stay sober," I stressed.

His thin face broke into a smile. He spoke softly. "Don't worry, Jack, you can depend on me!"

Few people looking at him would believe it, but I was optimistic as I climbed into a taxi.

I arrived for my appointment at the Sloane Tower punctually. It was certainly an easy way to gain experience of going abroad. Once inside the foyer, nobody looked English, neither could they speak it. Even the staff spoke with heavy accents. I was not sure where to go, so I approached the concierge. He took my name and pressed digits on a telephone. He nodded to instructions, then turned to a boy.

"Take Mr Whilloe to B6." .

I was led across the foyer, up stairs, through an arch and along a thickly carpeted passage. We were in the conference and business area. Eventually we stopped at a room and I was shown inside. It was fitted out for meetings, not too large. Against one wall was a small conference table covered in green baize and seating six. Against the opposite wall was a sofa. At each side of it were armchairs, flanking a low coffee table. There was a sideboard in front of the window, the top of which was clear, but which could presumably be laid out for drinks and snacks.

I took off my coat and threw it on one of the chairs. Shortly the door opened and a waiter appeared with a tray of tea. There were china cups and saucers, some sandwiches as well as small iced cakes and biscuits. I was asked whether I preferred milk or lemon. I chose milk. The waiter poured with a strainer. Like Hjørdis Foss, the Sloane Tower preferred leaf tea. I was handed the milk jug so as to serve myself with exactly the right quantity. The performance was impeccable. I could see what people paid for here. I reflected on the difference in quality between this and the tea bag in hot water at the café near Hatton Garden. I preferred this, but on the price difference, the tea bag was better value. When the waiter had seen me settled with a sandwich, he told me that he had a message from Miss Skillette to enjoy my tea. She would be with me in a few minutes as soon as a meeting concluded.

Why was everybody always in meetings? Ministers talked about cutting back red tape, but why not introduce a national meetings tax? The economy would surge forward.

Half an hour passed. I had another cup of tea, ate two more sandwiches and a sickly cake. I became impatient and began to pace the room. There was a telephone in the corner. I wondered whether it would be in order to ring and enquire, but I decided to leave such drastic action for another fifteen minutes.

I was looking out of the window at the passing traffic beyond the strip of well-kept garden when the door opened. A voice said, "I'm sorry to have kept you waiting. I'm Clare Skillette."

I turned to face the fake Davina. I was too surprised to say anything at first. She held out her hand. I hesitated.

"All right," she said, "I know how you must feel, but this will not be easy for me."

Not easy for *her*? She knows how *I* feel?

She poured herself tea, although by now I guessed it must be stewed. She took two sips and put down the cup. I stared at her. She said nothing. Damn, I wanted her to do the talking.

"Are you going to tell me what the hell this is all about?"

"How much do you know?" she asked, looking up at me.

I was studying her. She was not quite the same girl who had visited my office. She looked rather older this time, much more confident and assured. I suppose the innocent girl business was an act. Marketing and public relations were a sort of act, so her training probably stood her in good stead.

"I'd prefer not to say," I replied. "First, I'd like to know why you came to my office impersonating a woman who was later murdered, and persuaded me to get mixed up in a thoroughly unpleasant intrigue?"

She crossed the room to the sideboard and opened one of the cupboards to reveal a mini-bar.

"Would you like a drink?" she asked.

"Not for the moment."

She poured herself a gin and tonic.

"Let's sit on the sofa."

She was becoming nervous but did not lose her air of businesslike confidence.

"Until recently, Martin and I were lovers."

Oh God. What a stupid girl! Why him? She could have anyone!

"How did you meet him?"

"He contacted me after visiting my Aunt Dorothy."

Clare looked at me, but I said nothing. She went on to explain how her father owned the country headquarters of the Skillette clan and how the banished Dorothy had been allowed to rent one of the cottages in the village owned by the estate. As a little girl Clare liked her aunt and paid secret visits to her cottage, a process which continued throughout her adolescence and into her adult years.

"Did Dorothy put Martin onto you?"

"Oh no. She had already had her stroke by the time Martin saw her, but the matron mentioned my regular visits to him. I wasn't very difficult to trace and we met here for lunch. I found him attractive and... well, the usual story."

"How did you come to do this play-act in my office?"

She hesitated. This time I saw the frightened eyes that I had seen before. I could tell she was fighting back tears.

"Jack, I have been such a fool. I'm in deep shit... sorry, I mean, I am in trouble. Bad trouble."

"Never mind the language, just tell me the truth. The only way for us to get you out of your difficulty, whatever it is, is to get to that truth as fast as we can."

I was becoming irritated because disappointment was creeping over me. I was fairly sure that this girl was not Dorothy Skillette's child. There would have been no point in all the nursing home business if Dorothy had had the baby adopted by her own brother.

"Martin knew who you were and he said he wanted to get to know you. He has a rather strange way of thinking, but you have to remember he is very clever. It's his brain that invents all those security systems. His imagination is like a labyrinth. He thought he would be able to judge you better if you were investigating him, rather than the other way around. So he made all sorts of enquiries about you, read your book and articles, and then asked me to lure you to the village. Apparently he told Davina that he had asked you himself, so that the thing would tie up at both ends. He told me exactly what to say."

Why should this demented electronics genius want to get to know me? Still, I had better not interrupt this confession, so I said brightly, "Including the dinner invitation?"

"Yes."

"What the hell was I going to say when I saw his real wife?"

"He said he wanted to see your reaction, but if there were any problems he would fix it."

Fix it he certainly did.

"Did you understand that to include murder?"

"Of course not, but you must remember he saw you as a threat. He managed to persuade me that you were a threat. I thought I was in love with him at the time."

"So what happened when he killed his wife?"

"That was the point. He told me *you* had killed his wife, but that he couldn't prove it. He said you were very dangerous!"

"So how do you know I'm not?"

She was silent for a while.

"Because I have come to my senses. And then there was the alibi."

"What alibi?"

"Well, he had been at Beechurst on the morning Davina was murdered, but he thought that might look bad, so he asked me to confirm to the police that we were together at his flat off Cadogan Square."

"Did the police question you?"

"Yes, I made a statement."

"Did they ask you any questions about me?"

"No, you were never mentioned. They seemed more interested in Martin."

"So you told them that that Saturday morning you and Martin were in bed together at his flat, which was a lie?"

"Yes."

"You're certainly in shit, Clare. What about the Kapowski murder?"

"We have never discussed it. I've only read about it in the papers."

"Did you know Martin knew Kapowski?"

"No."

"Why should Martin see me as a threat?"

"Because of who you are."

"I'm not a threat. He's the threat! The person in his sights is Dorothy Skillette's child. To tell you the truth," I said over my shoulder as I walked to the fridge to get myself a whisky, "I thought up until today that Dorothy Skillette might be your mother."

There was a silence behind me. I turned around with my drink. Clare was looking at me in disbelief.

"But Jack, I thought you knew! Dorothy is *your* mother!"

CHAPTER THIRTEEN

There was a thud as the glass slipped through my fingers and onto the carpet. It is said that the moment your life is about to end your whole past flashes before your eyes. Something very like that happened to me then.

Clare ran towards me, took my arm and sat me in a chair. She poured me another drink.

"I'm terribly sorry. I had no idea. I thought you knew all along. Martin said that you did!"

As my mind cleared, a million pieces fell into place. Perhaps I had suspected this. There was something about the old lady. Of course it was my adoptive father who had collected the baby from the clinic.

Thoughts darted back and forth through my reeling brain. I said nothing. Clare sat opposite me, silent and watching. It was ironic that the girl who so recently had tricked me by concealing her own identity was the one whom fate had chosen to present me with mine.

"You and I are cousins," I said.

Clare nodded.

"You are the first blood relative I have met!"

"There's your mother."

"Yes, but I did not realise."

Clare nodded again.

All my life had so far had a strange and disconnected air. I was attached to other people's lives by invitation and legal documents. I had never sought to uncover my own beginning. But now, sitting here, knowing that I was connected by blood to people who were real, whose own lives provided material for the threads that made up my own, was as if I had suddenly become a person for the first time.

I think I could have sat there, silent and still, in the armchair in that little conference room for hours and hours, letting thoughts and memories wash over me, rearranging themselves into a new history and purpose, so as to re-establish my life set on a foundation, true and real. But another more compelling thought intruded, pressed by the urgency of survival. *I* was the target. Martin knew who I was. The nearer I came to the truth, the nearer I moved to the centre of his web, where that vile genius, his appetite for the taking of life aroused by his two earlier murders, sat waiting for me, his final victim, to present myself for sacrifice.

There was work to be done. I shook myself into action. First, I called the Iron Duke. Paddy was there and he sounded sober. I arranged with him to bring his car to the Sloane Tower, then take Clare to his girlfriend's flat and keep her there until he heard from me again. He gave me the phone number. I gave Clare specific instructions to lock herself in this conference room and let no one in until Paddy arrived.

"How will I know it's Paddy?" she asked.

"You will recognise him by his florid face and Irish accent."

Clare looked at me anxiously. "Jack, where are you going?"

"Don't worry about me. Remember, at the moment you are the one in danger, because you alone have the tangible evidence which can put Martin behind bars. That's why you must go into hiding."

Reluctantly, she acquiesced.

"You are in danger, too, Jack. Take care!"

Outside I wished I had the Morgan with me, but there were taxis available, so I hailed one and told the driver to take me to Lincoln's Inn. It was approaching six. I hoped Gerard would still be there. He usually was, because he drove to work and liked to leave after the traffic had subsided. I was in luck, but only just. I found him in his office clad in a dinner jacket. He was off to some do in the City.

"Goodness, St John, you keep popping in at awkward times!" Gerard peered at me. "Are you all right? You look a little worse for wear!"

I told him not to worry and that I did not have time to explain. Then I came to the point.

"Have you a set of my adoption papers in the safe?"

I took him off guard. His demeanour changed. He sat down behind his desk.

"After all these years, St John, why do you want to see them now?"

I waved his objections to one side impatiently. "Never mind. Just let me see them!"

Gerard looked uncomfortable. "I can't."

"Why not?"

"They were stolen."

"Stolen? What the hell do you mean?"

Gerard told the story. Apparently, about three weeks ago the partners' safe, which was inside the strongroom in the basement and contained the highly sensitive family papers of the individual partners own family affairs, was found open. A careful inventory with all of them revealed that the only item missing were the adoption papers.

"Were the police informed?"

"No."

"Why not?"

Gerard looked shifty again. The safe had been opened by someone who knew the combination; therefore it must have been one of the partners. I was livid.

"So which of you pinched the papers?"

"That's the point. None of us did." It seemed to me that Gerard was blushing. "We thought that you had taken them yourself."

I stood up, leant on his desk and pushed my face to within inches of his.

"And how the fuck could I open the safe if I didn't know the fucking combination?!"

Gerard winced. He hated foul language. It showed bad form.

"We thought you must have found it out."

I sat down again with an exasperated sigh. Why people paid money to use the brains of this bunch of fools was beyond me. Suddenly I had a thought.

"What sort of safe is it?"

"That's the point. It's a fairly new one."

"Yes, but what make?"

"MicSec."

I was out of the door before Gerard could say anything more, but halfway down the passage I remembered I had no car. I shot back to his office where I found him uncharacteristically wiping his hands on a silk handkerchief. They must have been sweaty with fright. He looked relieved as I came in again.

'Gerard I need a car. Can you lend me yours?'

"St John, just listen to me for a moment, please! We all of us knew that you were sensitive about your origins, which was evidenced by the fact that you didn't want to know anything about them. We thought you were making your own enquiries in your own way. Of course, I realise now we were wrong."

I let Gerard have his say. He told me that because it was a private adoption and no agency was involved, the documents had been prepared by *Whilloes*, and the ones which were stolen were copies.

"They were in a secure envelope sealed in wax by father. Only he knew the contents. They contain only the formal information confirming your adoption. I believe they identify your mother, that is all. If you want to have the full details of who you really are, you would have to refer to father."

Gerard drew on a cigarette. He clearly did not know that Dorothy Skillette was my mother, and he probably never heard of Titus Mynot. I decided not to reveal the revelation of my own identity until I had talked with Edward Whilloe.

I felt a compelling need to talk to my adoptive parents about my background before making the next move, which would have to be a confrontation with Martin Michener. I asked Gerard again if I could borrow his car. I fancied that if he were going to a boozy function it would be safer for him to take a taxi back to his pied-à-terre in Chelsea. He hesitated for a bit. Would I be able to drive it? What impertinence! Far more skill was needed to drive a Morgan than a Jaguar. Eventually he handed me the keys.

"You'll need this as well," he said, scribbling some figures onto a scrap of paper which he tore from a memo pad.

"You will have to feed those into the machine to raise the barrier to get out."

It was a little uncanny to move into the traffic in complete silence, with the strange sense of remoteness from the world outside. The big saloon had every refinement, including a mobile telephone. I used it to ring home and tell them I was on the way, although it would be quite some time. Ma sounded quite pleased. Messamer Hall was not far from Marlborough, but I had to break through the rush hour traffic onto the M4 and then make my way, bumper to bumper even in the fast lane, all the way to Wiltshire.

It was just after nine when I reached the house. It was quite as grand as its name sounded, a mansion, part Elizabethan. Added to and modernised as one century passed into another, it sits in a hundred acres of park and garden, a comforting array of gables and chimneys mellowed and timeless. Not much of this could be seen in the dark, but I knew it was there. The big saloon crunched its way to a halt in the gravel before the great oak front door. This swung open as I got out of the car. The Butler, Bentley, good name that for a butler, I wonder if there are any called Rolls, hovered to greet me.

'Good to see you Mr. Jack'

'And you Bentley! Where are my parents?'

He took my coat. 'In the drawing room. They have finished dinner. Would you like me to get you something?'

I thought for a moment.

'Bentley, this is a flying visit. I think I will have to go out again. Could you get cook to fix me some sandwiches and a flask of soup and put it all in the car outside?'

'Certainly Mr. Jack. I will see what can be done'

That was Bentley speak for Yes. I suppose I should have said earlier that I was about to enter a world where reality has given way to a pageant. The vast income from Whilloes plus the inherited wealth of my mother, from a cotton family which extended itself into coal and later oil, means that money flows as water from a tap. This enables my parents to live in the style of a period film. I ought to find it repellent. Yet somehow I struggle not to admire it.

I greeted Ma with the ritual kisses and Pa with a handshake and a pat on the shoulder. In the long drawing room, oak panelled since the Jacobites, we gathered around the fire. Ma, blue rinsed and exacting, her voice perfectly pitched into that annoying upper class drawl. Pa, less pretentious. Diffident, but shrewd. As a solicitor he acted for many of the great families. Anything commercial or international, or quarrels which were not connected with wills or divorces, he left to his partners. Even now in his mid-seventies he went to the office a couple of days a week. He stood perfectly straight and his hair and moustache, though grey in places, were far from white. Nancy and Edward Whilloe still made a very handsome couple.

Pa poured two whiskies with just a touch of soda. This was how he liked it, but in this environment it tasted just right. Ma never drank after dinner. She said it kept her awake. There was no point in beating about the bush. I told them the whole story.

They listened attentively and interrupted little. Ma grew more and more anxious, throwing up her hands in dismay as I told of the murders. I came to my new knowledge at the end. It was Ma who spoke first.

"It was never our intention to keep your identity a secret from you, although we had to keep it a secret from everybody else. But you seemed so disinterested. The time never seemed to be right." She sighed. "Perhaps we were wrong. Maybe we should have broached the subject to you. We so much wanted you to be a Whilloe, but it's obvious that you are a much freer spirit than any of us."

She laughed to her herself. "You have done us so much good. Without you, I think Gerry would have become impossible!" She always shortened my brother's name.

Pa had been looking thoughtful.

"I'm sure, St John, that you have now pieced together the fact that Dorothy Skillette was terrified of old Stanley Michener and his threats of vengeance. For this and other reasons, she felt she could not bring you up herself. We wanted a third child, so the arrangements seemed ideal."

He ran the tips of his fingers across his moustache. A gesture which I think was lifelong from when the whiskers first grew.

"Although you are passing through this distressing episode, I still think the decisions we all took for you were for the best. Now that the crisis which Dorothy feared has blown up, albeit in a most extraordinary and far-fetched way, you are much better able to deal with it."

I agreed with him. It was odd looking at them now. Although I had known, since I was quite young, that they were not really my parents, knowing now who my real parents were, I could see them in a much softer light. Their horizons were narrow and protected, and they had extended that protection to me.

Pa had left the room for a moment, I suppose to go to his study, and returned with a large envelope. It was sealed with wax and he handed it to me.

"You will find in there all the particulars of your background. In order to record it in a way that you would easily be able to understand, I have set out a narrative for you. I did it many years ago, intending you should read when you were ready. Now seems to be the time."

I opened the envelope and began to read. The words flowed into my mind and took meaning. I was stunned. It was several pages and took time. Ma rang for Bentley and ordered coffee, clearly no longer worried about being kept awake, and my father lit his pipe.

When at length and two coffees later I had finished reading I could think of nothing to say. There was a lot I *wanted* to say to these two old people who now watched over me so anxiously. They had taken me into their family from birth, believing I was threatened. They had given me the best of everything they had to offer, including their love. I had rewarded them with cynicism and rebellion. I felt confused and embarrassed. What could I say? What should I say?

My father spoke.

'Say nothing now. Let it all sink in. When you are ready, we will be here for you'

My mother added quickly,

'We love you Jack, no less than if you were of our blood. Keep that thought close to you always'

Without speaking I embraced them both. All our eyes were moist.

CHAPTER FOURTEEN

Getting a grip, I explained I must confront Martin. Not tomorrow but now. Hugging them both once more, I collected my coat from the arm of the omnipresent Bentley who had anticipated my plan and stood by the open front door. I sped off down the drive in the Jaguar, leaving a cloud of flying grit behind its spinning wheels. The gardener could rake it back in the morning.

The adrenalin was pumping through my system at high pressure, but still my heart was torn by the faces of those two old people, wide-eyed and anxious as I had left them. In spite of everything, they truly loved me as their own. I blinked again to clear opaque vision.

As I drove at high speed across the country in Gerard's magnificent car, I took stock. I was going to a confrontation with a maniac who could see no distinction between good and evil, and who was meticulously plotting my own destruction. To him, taking life ceased to have meaning after he had committed the act. As he had killed twice already, he would not hesitate with me. I thought carefully of all that Professor Tewkesbury had told me. I remembered the trauma I had felt when I first met Martin and of his strange, hypnotic personality.

Cocooned in the silence of the big car, as it gulped the miles with an easy hiss, I plumbed the reservoir of my own courage. Tonight I was going to need all of it, down to the very last drop. Recklessly, I pulled the car phone from its rest and punched in the number of The Grange. After several rings the frail voice of Elderflower quavered in the earpiece.

"Is Mr Michener in?"

"Indeed, Mr Whilloe, he is at home."

My heart skipped a beat and my mouth went dry.

"Tell him," I said, "that I'm on my way."

It was after midnight when I reached the village. I had stopped for just ten minutes somewhere south of the M4 corridor to have Bentley's soup and sandwiches. Most houses were in darkness, but at The Grange the porch light was on. The sinister bulk was smudged here and there with patches of yellow, showing that not all the household was yet asleep. I swung the car into the drive and pulled up outside the door. No furtive passage this time along the tradesmen's path. I mounted the steps of the porch, wiping my sweating hands on the oily coat. I hesitated at the bell-pull, and instead tried the door. It was open. Unlike its image in a horror film, it swung back silently on well-oiled hinges.

The great elk stared at me malevolently from its perch high in the vault of the hall. The feeble lights cast eddying shadows which left dark patches to act as cover for the lurking demons, which my overwrought imagination told me dwelt for sure in this frightful place. A shaft of brighter light escaped from the part open door of the library. Wide-eyed I made for this. It beckoned me forward to my confrontation with the twisted mind who sat within.

Yet, as I pushed open the door and entered, I found it empty. A fire burned in the hearth and there were papers, which looked like architect's plans, open upon the desk. My book was visible beneath the folds. I took off my coat, and dropping it on a chair, stood before the fire. As I did so, a cold blast of air caught my cheek. The curtains were open, and it was then that I noticed a pane of glass was broken and one of the windows was ajar. A gust of wind caught the window and caused it to swing back. I crossed the room and shut it securely.

At that moment I heard the metallic clatter of locks in the hall which I recognised as the front door being secured. I surmised this might be Elderflower. A soft and measured footfall moved steadily towards the library door, which swung back to reveal the master of this house of hell, Martin Michener. His hypnotic eyes shone in the firelight.

"My dear St John, you made good time."

He smiled at me. A chill exultant, grimace. He went on

"And why not? Empty roads of the night and the unlimited power of one of the world's great cars. I hope you enjoyed your drive!"

His tone was even, soft and menacing. Clenching my fists at my sides, I spoke, my voice pitched high with fear. "Martin, we have to talk."

"Talk? Yes. Talk! What fun. Talk lightens the soul!"

He crossed the room and drew the curtains.

"We need to keep out the draughts," he turned to me to finish his sentence with another of his leers "following your forced entry."

"Forced entry? What are you talking about? I came in through the front door which was open!"

"The front door is locked securely. This window is broken. Your fingerprints are on the latch. Footprints which will match your shoes exactly will be all over the flower bed outside. The evidence leaves no doubt."

In preparing myself on the journey from Berkshire, I had imagined a tempestuous, even violent, encounter. I was not prepared for slimy cunning.

"But I have not been walking in your flower bed!"

"No, but shortly your shoes will."

What was he talking about? I hate meaningless conversations.

"Martin, either we talk sense or just forget it. Pissing around with riddles does not appeal to me."

"Dear me, St John. You are so impatient. Let me explain. Your shoes will leave footprints because temporarily I will be wearing them."

"Not if I refuse to take them off!"

"You will be dead."

Ah! The duel of wits had begun.

"Whatever your scheme, if you kill me, sooner or later you will be caught!"

"I think not. Killing in self defence is not a crime, especially when one finds a ruthless and unprincipled killer, armed with a pistol, breaking into one's house."

This was ridiculous.

"I have no pistol."

"But my dear St John, you do! Here it is."

Martin withdrew his hand from his jacket pocket. He was holding a small pistol, a .22 Automatic.

"Unregistered and unlicensed. No one knows how you came by it. You will shoot first, but miss."

Martin walked to his desk and opened a drawer.

"Even if you had been a better shot, a small calibre pistol like that would probably do no more than give a painful wound. This, however, will kill you stone dead with a single shot." Martin waved a huge revolver, I think a Magnum. "I shall, of course, have to explain events to the police, but they already strongly suspect you for the murder of my dear wife and that unfortunate little engraver."

The room was swimming before me. I was overcome by the same feeling of oppression that I had felt here when I had come to dinner after Davina's murder. I struggled to get a grip of myself and to understand what was happening. I suspected Martin was employing some form of hypnosis. I caught sight of my book and concentrated on it. That was part of me. If I could hold my attention to it, maybe my mind would be able to resist the influence of this fiend. I tried to recall its contents, page by page. My head began to clear.

His voice taunted me.

"Not only are you a murderer, but a philanderer, too. The television presenter, such a charming girl. The innocent little widow, with whom you have made your temporary home so as to plot and spy and kill. Then, your latest interest, your cousin, Clare. Cousins should avoid conjunction with each other. It is said to produce idiots."

I should have hit him, yet my rage and disgust were not matched by strength. My limbs were weak. My arms hung limp. My legs struggled to support my weight.

"St John, my dear fellow, the night is still quite young. We have a lot to discuss before the curtain comes down on your experience of this earth. Let us have a drink."

He turned his back and opened a small cupboard in the corner of the room. I heard the ring of crystal. Both pistols were on the desk within easy reach. I knew what to do, but I found I had no will to do it.

Martin spoke without turning. "Do not worry. I know the guns are there, but you have no power to use them now."

He handed me a glass of whisky.

"I have added a little Malvern water. For the finest malts, it is, I think, best."

111

My tormentor sat behind the great desk. He raised his glass towards me.

"To your future, St John. It will be very short. But no matter. Eternity follows even for the wicked! A tormented eternity perhaps, but who knows?"

I struggled to regain control. I took a slug of the whisky. Perhaps it would help. Or was it poisoned? Maybe drugged? Too late. I had drained the glass. Where was the heroic figure who had leapt from his car, determined to bring this murderer to book? A lifeless wimp, at the mercy of his quarry. A mouse, mesmerised by the stare of the cat, which played gleefully with its victim before striking the fatal blow.

Martin was speaking. His voice echoed. Was it the drink? Or hypnosis? Or was it me? Was I losing my reason?

"Of course, once I had learned you were Dorothy's wretched child, I could have accosted you in a dark alley and pushed a knife between your ribs, but I wanted to learn more about you. I wanted to watch and observe what kind of person you were, how you would behave under pressure, whether you could be tempted by women. The sort of things which are such fun to know about another. After I had read your book, I realised that you were a skilful investigator, so I seduced your gullible cousin and engaged her innocence to lure you to the village where you would be in my power. Of course that is not how it will seem!"

Martin put his tumbler to moist lips and sipped.

'This is how it will be'

Another sip.

'Now that you had discovered who you were, you were determined to claim what you thought was yours. Framing me for crimes you were committing was clever as well as cunning."

Framing him! What a bastard! I fought to recover my wits. I must try and regain control of the conversation. I shot a question.

"Where did your wife, Davina, fit in?"

"What do you mean 'fit in'? She was *your* first victim. I hated her. She was a Mynot. I hate Mynots. They are a family cursed. I was overjoyed when you killed her!"

The question had helped. I felt a little strength returning. I tried another.

"Martin, why did you kill your wife?"

He looked at me with a quizzical smile. "Really St John, *you* killed her! Perhaps it was on impulse. Perhaps because she may have discovered who you were. Another Mynot!"

In my mesmerised confusion I was almost hallucinating, whether because of the failure of my own mind or the hypnotic power of Martin's, I had no idea, but in my lucid moments I could not help but admire this satanic man. He had all the answers at his finger tips, delivered in a soft, exacting voice through moist lips, as if feeding on them, like a voracious slug.

"What about Kapowski?" I asked.

"Just to make sure that your evil intentions were understood. After stealing documents from the safe in your firm which revealed your identity, your mind became unhinged, remember, and you went on a rampage of vengeance, terrible and wicked. Finally, you came here to kill me, but fortunately," he stroked the Magnum, "I am prepared." He spread his hands on the desk and sighed. "Thus will end a chapter of wickedness. Death is a great healer."

The vision of Jefferson Tewkesbury floated before me. I heard him warning me once again. Danger!

Something snapped. I found myself on my feet leaning on the front of the desk, bent forward to Martin and shouting.

"Stanley! Stanley Michener! Why are you doing this to me?!"

There was a moment's silence. A look of surprise on Martin's face.

Had I caught him unawares?

He hesitated. His head tilted slightly to the left. He seemed to be listening for a distant sound.

Then he responded. His voice had changed. It was no longer smooth and oily. It was harsh and angry.

"Because you are the evidence of a vile betrayal. You are the fruit of a violation of a Michener by a Mynot. No Mynot will ever lay its greedy hand upon the tiniest part of the fortune of the house of Michener!"

It was now or never.

"But Stanley!" I cried, "Martin is the Mynot. *I* am the Michener! Stanley, I am your grandson!"

I heard my words echoing round the room which spun before me out of control. They bounced off the walls and rang in my head at deafening volume. I collapsed back into my chair and closed my eyes. When I opened them he stood above me, leaning, with one hand on the desk. His expression troubled, his eyes dull, his frame shrunken, his features aged.

"What are you saying?"

Now was the moment. This mutated double mind must be forced to confront reality.

"Your young wife, Dorothy, was having an affair, but not with Titus Mynot. With your son, Arnold. *He* was the father of Dorothy Skillette's child. Your wife bore you your own grandson!"

He swayed and sank into the chair behind the great desk. Softly he murmured beneath his breath tortured, anguished words, "Not possible! Martin is a Michener!"

"No Stanley, you are wrong! Titus Mynot was indeed having an affair, but with Arnold's wife, Katherine. The baby she bore was his. It is Martin who is the Mynot. You must understand, Stanley, that Martin is no relation of yours whatsoever. You made a mistake. You inhabited the wrong baby, and when Martin grew up and unknowingly married his cousin, the whole Michener heritage was in the hands of Mynots!"

All this was true. I had read as much from Edward Whilloe's narrative. Except the spiritual exchange bit. Even now I could not be sure that such a thing had, or even could, happen. Maybe Martin's insanity took this form of delusion, but talking to him as Stanley was having its effect. Whether I was merely playing to his delusion or actually talking to Stanley was not important.

The person sitting before me put his head in his hands. When he looked up I knew for sure he had changed. Not the spectacular instant ageing of the horror film. The physical appearance did not alter, but the presence did.

Finally, he spoke. The voice was a whisper. "So all along you were the person I believed myself to be?"

"Yes. I am the Michener. You are the Mynot."

His eyes were a dark mixture of defiance and despair. A gust of wind billowed the curtains, yet now I was immune from the chill. I walked over to the cupboard and looked at the drinks. Among them was a bottle of vodka. I poured a generous shot and set it on the desk. He sipped it two or three times, then gulped it down in a single slug. I settled in the armchair, watching him closely. I did not know now whether I was faced by Martin or Stanley. I waited for a sign.

Yet, who was I? I had begun the day St John Whilloe, origins unknown but full of self-confidence. By early evening I was the son of Dorothy Skillette and Titus Mynot. But when I read my father's painstaking narrative, I found that the great secret had been Arnold's involvement with Dorothy. So now I was the only surviving Michener.

I looked at the figure behind the desk, and he stared back at me. I think at that moment we knew instinctively that the duel of wits was over. In the distance I became conscious of the wail of a police siren. It drew closer. Then I heard a second. Shortly, there was a great commotion as police vehicles came to a halt in the road outside. There was beating on the door and shouts of "Police! Open up!"

I could not draw myself away from the man behind the desk. There was the dull thud of heavy shoulders, shortly followed by the splintering of wood. Many footsteps. The door of the library flew open. What seemed several, but I think three, uniformed officers burst in, followed by Chief Inspector Bridgenorth. The inspector pushed forward.

"Martin Michener. I am arresting you for the murders of Davina Michener and William Kapowski."

Bridgenorth followed these dramatic words with the usual caution. Behind him loomed two more figures. Paddy and Clare. That explained it. She must have spilled the beans.

Martin shrugged but said nothing. He bent to pick up the plans which had been scattered across the desk earlier and which had fallen to the floor. Folding them neatly, he handed them to me.

"These are the plans for a new alarm system for The Grange. As you can see, the property is far from secure." He laughed. "It is often said that cobblers are the worst shod."

He took a step towards the waiting officers and stopped. He turned to me, smiling faintly, then I saw, we all saw, he held the magnum. Everyone froze. Clearly the officers were unarmed. A glaze passed across Martin's face. He remained standing for a few more seconds before putting the gun to his mouth.

Bridgenorth shouted and lunged forward

'No! Don't!

There was a deafening explosion. Brain tissue and fragments of skull splattered in a bloody montage over the wall behind Martin as he crashed to the floor.

I think I must have blacked out. I do not know whether it was from the shock, which was unlikely, or from the sudden rupture of some hypnotic trance, which was even more unlikely. No matter.

When I recovered, the scene before my refocused eyes was one of surreal confusion. Bridgenorth was bending over Martin's lifeless form with one of the uniformed officers. Another was speaking into a crackly radio calling for backup. Rosa was in the doorway screaming, supported by an ashen Joseph, mouth agape. Clare was vomiting into the waste paper bin, attended by Paddy.

I rose unsteadily from my chair, walked into the hall, pushing past the hysterical Rosa clutching her dumbstruck husband and out of the splintered front door. Leaving the Jaguar, I made my way on foot to my lodgings, let myself in quietly and crept up to my room. Stopping only to remove my shoes and jacket, I climbed into bed.

In a moment I was asleep.

In the morning I would wake up.

A new person to a new life.

Actually not much changed.

CHAPTER FIFTEEN

The rain stung my cheeks as I hurried down Greek Street in London's Soho. I was late. Late for lunch with Clare. I was also pissed off. I hate being late.

More than a year had passed since that freakish nightmare at The Grange. Much of it was jolly boring, so I will just give the main bits. The police wrapped up the case quickly. They let Clare off with warning not to get mixed up with dodgy people in future. I think that included me. I found I owned the entire Michener empire, which was a complete farce as my adoptive family stinks with money and I am included in its huge network of trust funds. Anyway I sold the whole company to a Japanese outfit for £120 million. Then I set up a Charitable Foundation to help the poor and the starving in Africa, run by some well known serial do gooders. I kept back a few million. Just in case of the unforeseen. I gave Paddy a tidy sum to keep him comfortable for the rest of his days, which if he does not curb the drink, may not be too many. I then had a look at the new life on offer, but it did not appeal, so I went back to my old life as if nothing had happened.

Rosa, Joseph and Elderflower were in a frightful state over Martin, but I cut them a deal and now they are happy. I let them stay at the Grange and arranged for Mrs Bulmer to run it as a second rest home. I moved Dorothy, I cannot call her my mother as I do not think of her that way, into her old room at the Grange and she is now looked after by Rosa, who runs the place under the supervision of a Matron. It is odd but Dorothy is definitely better, though she still cannot talk. I would like to ask her why she let them take her baby away. She was not some teenage prostitute after all. Surely she could have brought me up in that cottage? Did she mind losing me? Was she heartbroken? One day maybe she will be able to tell me. Till then it is better not to dwell on it.

Elderflower is now treated as a customer as he is too old for even his sort of work. I go down to Beechurst most weekends, but I stay with Susan. We continue to be lovers but I think neither of us wants to go further. When we are together we are together, but when we are apart we are free. I am useless at commitment. It did not work with Melissa. Mind you I am seeing Melissa again and when she is in the hetero mood and I fancy silk and everything just so, we spend the odd night together.

As I arrived damp and chilled at the entrance to Emilio's, my mind was on Clare. Emilio greeted me just inside the door. He is ageing now. His Latin looks, dark and smouldering, have given way to a grey but kindly twinkle. I had been coming to this place since I was a child. As always he was immaculate in his black bow and white tuxedo and as always he was effusive. He is one of the old style restaurateurs who greet their customers and run their business from the front where the diners are. Not like the modern breed of TV chef yelling obscenities in the kitchen, while oily fronters keep telling everyone to enjoy their meal.

He took me to my usual corner table. Clare, looking spectacular in a black roll neck with pearls, was already there sipping white wine. I bent to kiss her on the cheek. She tilted her head so that I connected instead to her lips. This was a good sign. We were still not lovers.

'I am desperately sorry to be late. I was arguing with Gerard!'
'How is Dorothy?'
'That's what the argument was about. Dorothy's fine and settled in, but I am not sure whether she knows where she is. I am sure she knows who I am. Anyway I have set up a Trust which now owns the Grange, with enough extra capital to maintain it, and I have made Rosa and Joseph life tenants, so that they will always have somewhere, even if they end up as customers for care like old Elderflower'
'Why the argument?'
Clare sipped her wine then pushed the glass to me 'this is on the house because you were late, so you may as well have some'
'Thanks. There was no problem over the Trust; it was the fact that I wanted the part of the capital to go to Susan and her daughter, when the whole Elderflower family are gone. Gerard said the capital should stay in the family'.
'Gerard is right!'
Clare was old money. Those people hang onto assets.

She was not too keen on Susan. Thought her too ordinary. That was what I liked about her. Susan I mean. Her ordinariness. She also had warmth. Melissa had style. Clare had class. It was this class thing that was pulling me towards Clare. I had tried to resist. But I knew now I was losing. I was feeling guilty. It was against all my principles.

We ordered from an attentive Emilio then talked and laughed a great deal as we ate simple Italian food, recipes refined over centuries of Mediterranean sunshine, untouched by the sticky fingers of designer cooks and sensibly priced. Over coffee I needed to get something off my mind.

'I never really thanked you for saving my life that night at the Grange. If you and Paddy had not gone to the police I think it is my brains that would have been blown out'

As soon as I said it I regretted my choice of words. I remembered Clare's head in the waste bin. Fortunately she was unfazed.

'Forget it. I felt guilty that I had lead you into the trap in the first place'

She stopped talking for a moment and stirred her coffee. After a moment she carried on

'There was something really odd about Martin. He was, I am not sure how to put it, hypnotic. I was utterly in thrall to him but as soon as he was dead I could not imagine what I saw in him. It was really peculiar!'

So Clare had spotted it too. I wondered whether to embark on Aggressive Spiritual Exchange. I decided against. I had been to see Professor Tewkesbury and he was very excited when I told him the tale. He took lots of notes. I still think it bunk. Anyway I had a pleasant tea and another piece of Hjordis's chocolate cake. We parted on the warmest terms. Hjordis gave me a kiss on each cheek. I think she liked beards. I got the feeling that there might be more than cake on offer.

'I know what you mean. I had some very odd vibes when I was with him. Anyway' I smiled 'I owe you for that night'

Clare sipped her coffee.

'Maybe its time to pay'

I did not think she meant the lunch check. Our knees met under the table. I looked at her.

'What time do you have to be back at work?'

'I took the afternoon off'

As she said this she held my gaze.

'I'll get the bill' I said

I drained my glass, then I caught Emilio's eye.

To hell with my principles.

www.ingramcontent.com/pod-product-compliance
Lightning Source LLC
Chambersburg PA
CBHW050802250626
47155CB00005B/2181